D1290136

JOHN EAX

and

MAMELON

Albion W. Tourgée

LITERATURE HOUSE / GREGG PRESS
Upper Saddle River, N. J.

Republished in 1970 by
LITERATURE HOUSE
an imprint of The Gregg Press
121 Pleasant Avenue
Upper Saddle River, N. J. 07458

Standard Book Number—8398-1967-6
Library of Congress Card—70-104584

Printed in United States of America

ALBION WINEGAR TOURGEE

Albion Winegar Tourgée was born in Williamsfield, Ohio, in 1838. Some of his ancestors were Huguenots who fled from France to the Western Reserve after the revocation of the Edict of Nantes, and others came to America on the *Mayflower*. He briefly attended the University of Rochester, but dropped out and took a job teaching school in Wilson, New York. In 1861 he enlisted as a private in the 27th New York Volunteers, and lost an eye in the First Battle of Bull Run. He was discharged, but re-enlisted the next year, this time as first lieutenant in the 105th Ohio Volunteers, and was again seriously wounded. Resigning from the Army in 1864, he set up law practice in Greensboro, North Carolina. Two years later, Tourgée was a delegate to the Southern Loyalist Convention in Philadelphia, where he courageously spoke out for Negro suffrage, and expressed his fears of acts of violence by former Confederate soldiers. Tourgée's speeches earned him the hatred of North Carolina's Governor Jonathan Worth, who called him "the meanest Yankee who has ever settled among us." Tourgée's life was threatened, and he was forced to carry sidearms.

In 1867 he founded the *Union Register,* a newspaper devoted to the policies of the Radical Republicans — the exclusion of Confederates from office being only one of the many unpopular opinions contained in his editorials. The *Register* lasted six months. In 1868 the "Ohio carpetbagger" was appointed judge of the Superior Court of North Carolina, where he heard the many complaints against the Ku Klux Klan, accusations which he later published in his exposé *The Invisible Empire.* Numerous attempts were made to remove Tourgée from his post, but apparently he was astute enough to cultivate powerful political friends who kept him in power. He was, however, forced to resign from the Board of Trustees of the University of North Carolina.

It is amazing that the Klan never killed Tourgée. He was revered as a protector of the Negro and the more liberal elements — especially teachers — among the whites, but the rich planters, as well as the "white trash," would have welcomed his assassination, and very likely discussed it on more than one occasion.

The hostility towards this physically frail but heroic man grew so strong that, soon after Grant had appointed him Pension Agent at Raleigh, he was forced, for the first time in his life, to flee the battlefield. Before doing so, however, he had instituted various social reforms, particularly in prison administration, prepared a Code of Civil Procedure, compiled a Digest of Cited Cases, and published, anonymously, the "C" letters, important contributions to North Carolina political literature. Despairing of the possibility of reconciliation between the North and the South, he went to New York, and became founder and Editor of a weekly magazine called *The Continent* (1882 - 84). He continued to write political articles, as well as novels which explored and occasionally proffered solutions to the terrible social evils of which he had first-hand knowledge.

In 1880 he campaigned for his childhood friend, James A. Garfield, who, from the White House, wrote to Tourgée saying that he "did not think my election would have been possible" without the influence of books such as *A Fool's Errand* and *Figs and Thistles.* Shortly before his assassination, Garfield invited Tourgée to confer with him on the subject of providing federal education for the South, a project which Tourgée had advocated for many years in speeches, articles, private conversations, and books. By the end of his life, however, Tourgée had abandoned the idea that education would ease racial tensions. He spent his last few years as Consul at Bordeaux, France, and died there in 1905.

Upper Saddle River, N. J.   F. C. S.
October, 1968

John Eax

and

Mamelon

OR

THE SOUTH WITHOUT THE SHADOW

By ALBION W. TOURGEE, LL.D.

LATE JUDGE SUPERIOR COURT, NORTH CAROLINA. AUTHOR OF
"A FOOL'S ERRAND," "BRICKS WITHOUT STRAW,"
"FIGS AND THISTLES," ETC.

NEW YORK
FORDS, HOWARD, & HULBERT

813
T727j JMᶜ

201089

TO

The New South

THAT IS TO BE

WHEN THE FIRE OF SELF-SACRIFICE SHALL HAVE BURNED AWAY
THE DROSS OF THE PAST AND LEFT ONLY ITS

Gold,

THIS BOOK IS EARNESTLY AND HOPEFULLY DEDICATED BY THE

AUTHOR.

John Eax.

CONTENTS.

JOHN EAX.

MAMELON.

PREFACE.

THE two stories that compose this volume are printed in this form because I love them. Almost a decade has passed since they were written. I feel old while I read the proofs, as if looking upon a swift-grown child. I have not changed them—I could not. To me they are parts of a great panorama which I tried to paint with the whole vast scene outspread before me. To change a part would mar the harmony of the whole.

I was first impelled to attempt the field of romantic fiction by the weird fascinations of Southern life. Thrown while yet young and impressible into the very vortex of the Reconstruction Era, with the sound of the bugle yet in my ears, the breath of battle hardly blown away from the field of strife, with the shadow of Slavery passing slowly over the land on which it had rested so long and so heavily, I walked amid the strange incongruous elements around me, as one in a dream.

The shadow was over all—the shadow of Slavery and of its children, Ignorance and War and Poverty. In the shadow I wrote, contrasting it with the light. It came to me then, almost as a revelation, that the North and the South were two families in one house—two peoples under one government; each believing that it thoroughly understood the other, and—resting in that belief—becoming hourly more and more estranged.

So I wrote, until the pages grew into volumes, and the thoughts which were once my own—the impalpable companions of my day-life and dream-life — entered into other hearts, and became the common property of mankind. I meet them here and there, and recognize them in strange new garbs. They masquerade before me in others' lives and words, and I sometimes smile at the antics of the winged truants whom I would not recall even if I could. I do not judge them, I cannot. I believe they have made some lives better and none worse, and with that I am content.

But there were rifts in the shadow, some of
which I tried to paint. These stories are two of
them.

Perhaps I love the little waifs all the more because of the circumstances under which they were
written. On one occasion I had listened until
well past midnight to the tales of an inexhausti-
ble *raconteur* who dwelt with a peculiar delight
on the traits and deeds of a strongly marked old
family, whose seats of power had been in sight
of the county town where we were. The next
day these strange tales seemed echoing in my
ears amid the routine business of a country court.
Among the parties who were that day before
the court was one whose quaint name somehow
became entangled in my mind with these traditions. When I went to my room in the country
inn that night, I found a page of my " Judge's
Minute Book" closely covered with the cabalistic
words " John Eax." I hardly know how it came
about, but the queerly-named suitor and the proud
old family seemed to affiliate wonderfully well in
spite of their diversities of antecedent; " *John Eax*"
and the " *De Jeunettes*" kept company with me all
the night, and as the morning broke I filled the
last page of my " docket" with the closing words

of the story. It was a queer " record " to be
"made up" there, and I could but laugh at the
odd admixture of fact and fiction in the conse-
crated domain of law; but as I drew aside the
white muslin curtain and saw the autumn morning creep up the flame-lit slopes of "*Beaumont*,"
I felt that I had been a not ungrateful listener to
the genial tale-teller of the old *régime*.

One day in the spring of 1874, while holding
term in a neighboring county, there happened to
be no business ready to be taken. Adjourning
till the next day, I wandered off to an old church-
yard, neglected and forlorn, with the red tongues
of numerous gullies bearing fiery testimony of the
unthrift around, but having in one corner a cedar-
sheltered nook where an old flat tablet showed
above a luxurious bed of clambering blue-eyed
periwinkle. I picked the moss dreamily out of
the old-time lettering, deciphered the quaint inscription, and transcribed it in my pocket-diary,
sitting there among the periwinkle and using the
gray old tablet for a desk. The sun shone
brightly; the mocking-bird swung on the top-
most branch of the cedar and sang. There I
wrote the first chapters of "*Mamelon*" in my note-
book.

The two stories give glimpses of the Reconstruction Era at the South, without the shadow that hung over the land. If the North and South are contrasted, it is but to show the fusing potency of love or the solvent power of manly friendship.

Should others take half the pleasure in reading that I have enjoyed in preparing this little volume, I shall be amply repaid.

ALBION W. TOURGEE.

New York, Oct. 7th, 1881.

JOHN EAX.*

CHAPTER I.

UNDER DURESS.

"JOHN EAX." It was an odd name, but somehow it looked strangely familiar, and as I sat with the book open before me I read it over listlessly time after time with a dim struggling sense of recognition.

Almost unconsciously I traced, as well as my numbed brain would allow, the events of my life, striving to recall in what connection I had heard or seen the name, *John Eax*. My memory for names had always been bad. I could never cite cases by name and page from memory like other practitioners of the law. But my power of association was unusually good. Given a name,

---

* Pronounced with the sound of long ē,—— *Eex*.

place, or idea, I could almost invariably bring up the correlative or associated impression. So, while I could not remember names, if a name was once associated in my mind with a face, the one would usually recall the other. If I saw the countenance, I could generally remember the name, or if I saw the name it would bring up the countenance.

I soon became satisfied that I had never met John Eax in person, as I had no recollection of his individuality. Yet I could not keep my mind from running on it idly and vainly as the long hours of the summer afternoon crept away, and the evening sun threw his scorching rays through the one uncurtained window of the room in which I sat. The window was high up from the floor, and as the sunlight fell upon the rough pine table before me it was broken into many small squares, separated by broad frames of shadow. It was the first time I had ever noticed such a shadow, and I remember thinking it odd that I had never thought of the phenomenon before. It was my first day in Childsboro' jail. I had lived in sight of it all my life. I had visited clients many a time in this very cell which I then occupied. Yet never once had the thought occurred to me that the very sunshine was made to wear shackles, to the eyes of the unfortunate prisoners.

I was alone—except for the rats and vermin who rioted amid the filth of the ill-kept prison. In those days humanity was little studied in the construction or care of jails. As much of discomfort, deprivation, and suffering as could well be crowded between four walls was considered, in this region at least, an indispensable attribute of a perfect prison. The constitution of the State of North Carolina forbade "cruel and unusual punishment." No man dared lay the prisoner on the rack or pull out his nails with hissing pincers; but while the poor wretch waited for his trial in the jail, the frost might loosen his joints and cripple his members, or the summer sun might heat the fetid atmosphere in that steaming caldron of a cell until every breath was to the panting breast like the fumes of hell to the doomed soul. No extraneous cause of suffering could be applied to the prisoner in the jail, but every essential of health and comfort might be removed, and it was the general notion that they should be. Punishment, in those days, was inseparably associated with suffering—physical pain. The gallows, the lash, and the branding-iron were its implements, and it was considered eminently proper that they should be supplemented by disease and exposure.

What right had the prisoner to complain? He should not have been weak or unfortunate or guilty if he did not wish to suffer. Was he not the scapegoat upon whom society had laid its hands and its sins? Of course it was a Christian law and in a Christian land.

You think that was long ago, but it was only yesterday. There was never any provision for warming the prisons of the State, except the debtors' rooms of the jails, until since the war, and there are not a few now who believe that a great backward step was taken when even this concession was made to the humanitarianism of the age. I have had clients who were frostbitten in the jail we see yonder, and know of many a poor fellow who has been as certainly murdered by consumption, pneumonia, or other diseases generated by exposure and filth and foul air and lack of exercise, as if a dagger had pierced his heart.

But I was in the debtors' room, and alone. Unusual privileges were granted me. I had one splint-bottomed chair with a back and one without, a pine table of ordinary dimensions, lavishly carved and ornamented by the generations of unfortunates who had been the tenants of the cell before me. There was a bed, the clothing of which had been white, and the odor of which suggested the thought of contagion. It was deemed, however, a very luxurious bed for one who chanced to be in my unfortunate condition in those days of prosperous ease. Besides these luxuries there was a water-bucket and a drinking-gourd. The jailer came three times a day with my meals, and did not fail to remark that mine was a very comfortable lot. Indeed, he seemed to regard my situation with something akin to envy. To be fed without labor, to sleep with-out need of waking, and to spend the day without thought for to-morrow was evidently to his mind the *ultima thule* of human blessed-ness.

Ever since he had brought me at noon the food which sat untasted on the other end of the table, I had been saying over and over again to myself:

"Eax—Eax—John Eax! where have I seen or heard or known that name?" I could not recog-nize the handwriting, and yet each letter seemed to have been burned into my brain. I tried to analyze it, to see if its characteristics would not aid me in identifying its owner. The letters were of medium size, but wonderfully distinct and firm. It was written before the days of gold or steel pens, and had all those ear-marks of mood and character which only the flexible quill could convey.

I had been somewhat accustomed to the study of handwriting, especially as an index of character. Among my professional acquaintances I was regarded as something of an expert in chirographic science, and had not unfrequently made wonderfully correct deductions from a bit of writing shown me for the first time, as to the writer's age, occupation, character, and habits. It was before the days of those experts who, with microscope and camera and minimetric gauge, have sought to reduce this science to a certitude. I had never thought of applying the formulæ of the higher mathematics to the chances of recurrent forms. I trusted only to the subtleties of an eye trained to observe the variant characteristics of chirography and the deductions of a brain that had always been fond of curious speculation. Applying this skill or knowledge, I endeavored to

picture to myself the personality of the man who
had written that name—

JOHN EAX.

It was firm, full, confident; there was not a stroke
too many, and no letter was neglected from taste
or carelessness. It had little of what is termed
"slope"—that is, its letters were nearly perpen-
dicular with the line of direction of the words.
The manner in which the letters were joined together or run into each other showed that they
were made with what is now known among pro-
fessors of the chirographic art as a "partial arm-
movement."

This was unusual in the handwriting of the old
days when I knew this must have been written,
but I had noticed that a certain conformation of
the hand not unfrequently compelled the adop-
tion of this method of letter-formation even in
those days of deliberate penmanship. I started,
then, from this premise. This was my horizon,
against which I was to project the personality of
John Eax, viz.: he had a short, thick hand, with
full, fatty fingers.

I concluded, further, that the writer was not
young, as there was no sign of immaturity or

indecision about the signature or any letter of it. It was equally certain that he was not old, as there was none of that sharpness of angle, heaviness in the downward or tremulousness in the upward strokes, one or the other of which indications I had always remarked in the chirography of old age.

John Eax was therefore in the prime of life, and from the firmness and decision of his hand more likely to be verging upon age than bordering upon youth. The title-page of the volume, on the fly-leaf of which the name was written, bore the imprint date ˙of 1745 — one hundred years before the time I first saw it; and the writing did not seem to belong to a much later period. Presuming it to have been within fifty years of that date, and taking the character of the handwriting into the account, I was satisfied of another and most important fact in regard to the personality of this sphinx of my imagination—to wit: John Eax was not a professional man. The training required for any of the learned professions of that day would have left a mark on the hand of any man which would have been unmistakable and ineradicable. So this became another item in the verdict I was making up in regard to this mysterious unknown :—not liberally educated.

At the same time, the evident ease, certainty, and smoothness of his chirography showed that the writer was not only accustomed to form this signature, but that his hand was by no means unfamiliar with the pen. It showed, too, a flexibility of finger and wrist which was inconsistent with the actual, daily pursuit of any manual avocation. I was of the opinion, also, that the style of the writing—*i.e.*, the manner of forming the letters and of joining them so as to make words— was the result not so much of any system which he had been taught, or training he had received, as of a necessity which had evoked it from himself. It was near enough to the conventional forms not to be usually deemed odd or strikingly peculiar, and yet far enough removed from them to be original. This, with the simple directness and total absence of anything like flourish or extraneous lines, showed a man of independent mind and easy circumstances.

So I added to my special verdict the following items:

1. Not engaged in any manual occupation at the time this signature was written. 2. Accus-

tomed to write, but neither a clerk nor a scholar.
3. In easy or affluent circumstances. 4. Accustomed to the exercise of authority—perhaps command.

As a whole, then, John Eax stood forth to my
mind a man of mature age and rather full habit;
with energies unimpaired by age or indulgence;
accustomed to obedience in others, and having
the characteristic spirit of the well-to-do Englishman, in that he cared little for others' opinions
of his acts so long as they were not in themselves
actually discreditable. But when I had thus con-
jured up before my mind's eye the gruff, gray-
whiskered Englishman of a century before, well-
clad and well-fed, vivid as the picture was I could
not recognize it, nor could I go any further in my
deductions. I had learned all that the signature
could tell me.

As I looked up in despair, the cross-barred
sunshine on the opposite side of the cell awoke
me from the half-unconscious stupor in which I
had been ever since my incarceration, and in
which I had pursued the dreamy, fruitless inquiry
which I have detailed. I have often thought
that it was a blessed thing, apart from other results, that my mind ran off into this hopeless

labyrinth which led nowhere except away from the agony and misery which surrounded my life. If something had not relieved the tension of those terrible moments I must certainly have died of sheer agony of soul.

The shadow of the cell window cast on the blank wall waked me from my dream. Its red flickering light and the black bars of shade reminded me of an old picture I had once seen, in which the condemned are represented as held down by adamantine bars—crossed and riveted like these—at which they gnashed and strained incessantly, while the flames of eternal torment swelled and seethed unceasingly beneath and about them. It was the very perfection of the old, medieval, monkish idea of hell. I remembered shuddering with horror when I looked on the original. Now I laughed at the painter's conception as puerile and weak. My own agony was so much fiercer and keener than that typified by this flesh-scorching hell, that I could mock at such mere physical ill. I would even have changed places with one whose drawn, pinched face, instinct with the smart of endless burning, I remembered then was pressed wildly to an opening of the grating which he clutched.

CHAPTER II.

A PROUD FAMILY.

MY family was one of the richest and proudest in the State. It had been clustered about Childsboro ever since the old colonial days. The sons and daughters of each generation, being usually few in number, had intermarried with the wealthiest of our neighbors, and settled about the old home-seat until there was scarce an influential family in the country which was not akin to us. Our family pride was of that self-sufficient kind which did not seek alliance with any more influential or powerful connection, because it did not admit that any such did, or could, exist. To be a De Jeunette was enough. There could be nothing more. The tradition of Huguenot extraction, sufficient wealth, and an absolute power to bind or loose, kill or make alive, in the county of Erle, constituted our house one of the princely families which the system of slavery built up and strengthened. It might have rivals, but would admit no superiors.

My father had two brothers, and one sister who had married a Fourshee. They were all settled upon the four eminences which stand like guardians at each cardinal point about the pretty, peaceful, scattered little town of Childsboro', which lies embowered between them. These seats were known as Highmont, Belmont, Graymont, and Beaumont, my father's home. Each was in sight of all the others, though they are more than five miles apart; and on any pleasant day, by hanging out a signal flag from the window of one of the old mansions, the whole brood of uncles, aunts, and cousins could be gathered there for dinner, or any other entertainment, in little more than an hour.

It was a beautiful sight when they would all come — the elders in their carriages with their black servants, fat and sleek with the easy jollity of their race; and the children, boys and girls, the grown ones on splendid blooded horses, and the younger ones on the tough and docile " Banker" ponies of the low country, with grooms and outriders, all laughing and shouting and racing to see who should first arrive.

We were a strangely united family, too. Uncles and aunts, nieces and nephews and cousins—by

numberless removes—we were all De Jeunettes.
There were no discords, no quarrels or heartaches,
in our circle. It was a saying in the country, that
if you touched one of us you stirred the whole,
like a swarm of bees. The individual members of
the family were not much given to outside friendship, but to be the friend of one was to secure the
devotion of all. In like manner, to be the enemy
of one was to have the hatred of the whole.

We were not given to broils or difficulties, but
woe betide the man whom the De Jeunettes settled upon to hate. Their revenge was a thing
certain to be counted on, and I fear the forms of
law rarely stood in the way of its accomplishment.
Of course it was done fairly, as the saying then
was; but a broil is easily provoked, and the De
Jeunettes were cool-headed and strong-handed.

Despite our somewhat convivial habits, we were
little given to excesses of any kind. Within our
own family it was one great feast from the year's
inning to the ending. It was rare that a day
passed when we did not all meet. If there was
sickness in one family, we went every day to
show our sympathy; and as soon as convalescence
set in, our family gatherings were held there until
the invalid was able to go out, and then he was

not allowed to return home until fully restored.
We drank, but it was with each other; gambled,
but it was with our cousins; bet upon the speed
of our horses, but the wagers came back as presents. Brawling and carousing, with their attendant ills, were the chief evils of the day and country, but they seldom affected a De Jeunette.
There *was* a tale, whispered from one to another
of the younglings, of one of the connection who
had so far forgotten himself as to herd with the
low-down trash which congregated in and around
Childsboro'. But the De Jeunettes stuck to him
as if the old *noblesse oblige* of other days rang in
their ears continually. They did not quarrel with
him because he gambled and fought—nor even
because he fell drunk and lay in the gutter, while
his horse came home riderless, and the ragged ur-
chins of Childsboro' laughed and threw mud at the
Lord of Beaumont, as my grandfather was called.
It was told, too, that when his excesses had impaired his estate, and his outlying plantations
were mortgaged, and even Beaumont threatened
with execution, the De Jeunettes did not fail him,
but came promptly to his aid, assumed his debts,
and when he had sown his wild oats and promised reform, burned his obligations and left his

inheritance unincumbered. He was a De Jeunette.

Once when a Judge of more than ordinary
nerve was riding the circuit, and my ancestor for
some drunken freak was committed to jail for a
contempt of court, there was a sudden mustering
of forces, and before the Judge had left the
bench, the jail was broken open and the prisoner
set at liberty. It was done in broad, open day,
and every one knew the culprits. They were the
De Jeunettes. The Judge—himself a fearless
man—ordered the arrest of the whole family, at
least its males ; but the Sheriff reported himself
unable to execute the process with the power of
the county, and the week of the term having
expired, the Judge reported the matter to the
Governor, and went on his way around the
circuit. The Governor, being largely indebted to
the favor and influence of the family, and mind-
ful of the future, found it quite convenient to
ignore entirely the application for aid.

It was told too, that another one of the old
stock was tried for murder. I did not learn the
particulars till long afterwards. I only knew then
that the family stuck to him faithfully, that by
some means a verdict of "not guilty" was com-

passed, and the honor of the family saved. And
it was whispered among the boys and girls—for
there was no sex in the cousinhood of the De
Jeunettes : the girls were as bold of heart and as
firm of hand as their brothers—it was told among
them, that there was some sort of an agreement
entered into by which the others became sureties
for his confinement as a dangerous lunatic, and
that the square, tower-like building, made of
brick, with odd, narrow windows, which stood in
the gorge where Black Creek burst through the
low mountain range that skirts Beaumont on
the north, was his prison for many a year. Not
till I came to practice at the bar myself did I know
how true was this grim tale.

It was no wonder that we were a proud old
family, nor that we enjoyed to the utmost our
wealth and distinction. Our very faults were
such as tended to unite us closer and intensify
our pride. It was a wonder that any one coming
of such a stock, and with all these traditions of
faithfulness and exclusion whispered into his ear
from infancy, should ever so far forget them as to
dream of mating with any of the common herd.

It was bad enough for a De Jeunette to think
of marriage with a family not previously akin to

his own. There were the Hauxtons, the Four-
shees, and the Dargans (corrupted from D'Ar-
gent), and other families that were allied to us
already, and which were held to furnish a sufficient field for selection by the young De Jeunettes
of either sex. We were not given to the process of
intermarriage between close relatives, by which
the strength and vigor of the original stock might
be impaired, as the stalwart frames and inflexible
wills of our family fully attested ; but it was a
sort of dogma among us that by intermarriage
with a few strong, select races, continued with
discretion and care, both fortunes and families
might be improved. By this means it was
thought that the peculiar excellences of the old
stock might be preserved, without any abatement
of their vigor or decay of their traits. This was
not openly announced as a canon of conduct in
the family, but was an idea which came to be
acted upon as rigidly as if the law of the land had
prescribed it. No De Jeunette looked forward to
marriage except among the more or less remote
cousinage of the family—and this was true of
girls as well as boys. Every belle of our especial
circle introduced into it a remoter cousin, and
every young man appropriated to himself a mate

from some outlying group of relatives. Thus we became a system of families of which the De Jeunettes were the centre, held together by a constantly increasing centripetal force.

Occasionally there would arise a more than usually self-willed scion of the old stock, who would persist in breaking over this rule and going outside of the charmed circle for a bride; but this—though always strenuously opposed—was never a *mésalliance*. They had always married into the highest families in this or the neighboring States. It was disapproved because it was not considered advisable to increase the connection; the De Jeunette idea being that a small connection well compacted was better than a large one loosely held together. So there had been, up to my time, no instance of one who had absolutely made a *mésalliance*. I was fated to break that rule.

It is not possible for one at this day to understand the enormity of my offence. There was a threefold aristocracy at that time—an aristocracy of blood, of wealth, and of slaves. The mere slaveholder was the lowest grade of aristocrat; the wealthy slaveholder was the next higher; and he who could point to a long or peculiarly distinguished ancestry as well as a slave-roll of especial length, was the last and highest grade of ante-bellum Southern aristocracy. Of this class the De Jeunettes were *la crême de la crême.* The very lowest of these classes was infinitely above the highest of the rabble below. It is true there were differences even there—small planters and tradesmen and mechanics honorable enough, but low; and overseers and "croppers;" and, last of all, the poor white trash, who well deserved their name.

All these latter distinctions were utterly immaterial to a De Jeunette as regarded marriage. It would have been unendurable to think that one of them should marry even the heir of a few slaves—into the class of the mere slave-owner. Below that, it was but a choice of tainted fish to the De Jeunette nostril.

In this undertow of nothingness I found a bride.

CHAPTER III.

"THE CEDARS."

I CANNOT tell how it came about. I was twenty-four years old; had graduated with distinction at the university, and, somewhat against the wish of my parents (or rather, I should say, of my family, for they had no will except what was merged in the collective volition of the De Jeunettes), had prepared for and been admitted to the bar. They had yielded to me in this, though no De Jeunette had ever before condescended, so far as was known, to learn or practise any trade or profession since one of our remote ancestors, landing at Charleston in the ante-revolutionary days, had modestly written his name upon the registry of the port, "Louis De Jeunette, *cordouannier*," in the quaint old French of his native province. I am not sure but they yielded to me in this the more readily, because I had seen that registry with my own eyes, and had come back, after my youthful attempt to ascend the family tree, and in a solemn conclave of all

the De Jeunettes had informed them of the startling fact that our primal knight was armed with
an awl ; that our great ancestor was a John Mar-
tel, of the Order of the Lapstone ; in short, that
we were a race of *shoemakers !* I do not think
they would ever have consented that I should
study for a profession but for my knowledge of
this dangerous family secret.

I was so unfortunate as to be ambitious. It
was not sufficient for me to be simply a De Jeunette. I wanted power : not merely that of
wealth, ownership—the power of vast estates and
ample possessions. I wanted some of that which
rules and governs men. I did not care for slaves :
I wanted followers, adherents, partisans—a client-
elage in the old Roman sense. They said I was
an innovation myself, or the result of one, because
my father, after almost endless negotiations and
beseechings, had obtained leave to extend the De
Jeunette connection by marrying Mary Neal, the
splendidly dowered and beautiful daughter of one
of the most active and influential families in the
State. Her Irish blood seemed to have set the
blue Breton drops into a sudden. ferment in my
veins. They acknowledged me to be a De
Jeunette of the De Jeunettes, in all but one

thing:—I could not follow peacefully the old ruts.

Yet I was a favorite with the whole host of kindred, and, almost from my earliest remembrance, it had been tacitly understood and accepted that the very flower of our whole family—the queen of the De Jeunettes, the black-eyed, heavy-browed, ruby-lipped Louise of Belmont—was to be my bride when, in the fullness of time, we should see fit to enter into matrimonial bonds.

We had never spoken to each other of love, but in our childish games we had played at man and wife ; as we grew older we had been more intimate than any of the other cousins, and something of that idea of ownership and self-appropriation which accompanies marriage had grown up between us.   I was her almost invariable attendant in all our excursions, and she fashioned her life to meet my engagements and wishes.   I knew that she loved me.   Her great dark eyes lost their haughtiness and became soft and tender when they looked into mine.   I did not doubt but that I loved her in return.   Indeed I had determined after due meditation that I would make a formal declaration, and consummate the expected union when I should have won a sufficient practice at

the bar to afford a support for bride and groom,
aside from the family revenues. Strangely enough
I was bound to live on the fruits of my own labor.
I would offer myself to our queen, as a knight
who had won his spurs in battle. She knew my
ambition and shared it fully, and her voice and
influence—by no means slight in the family circle—had been one agency by which had been
smoothed the way for the innovation I had made,
in my devoting myself to a profession.

One vacation I went to spend a few weeks in
hunting at an outlying plantation of my father's
on the river. While there I saw a vision. It is
needless to attempt a description of Alice Bain.
She was fairer than the summer sky mirrored in
the mountain lake. Slight as a fairy, with a wealth
of soft brown hair that caught the sunbeams in its
coils and stole their golden glinting; with tender,
shrinking eyes of changing blue, and lips that invited the tale of love before her tongue could
have syllabled its alphabet. But I wrong her to
attempt description.

I learned two things at once, which gave me
almost equal pain. I did not love my cousin
Louie, and did love Alice Bain, *the niece of my
father's overseer !*

It was too incredible for me to believe. I flew back to Childsboro' without speaking of my new discovery to any one, unless my eyes revealed it to the object of my sudden passion.

I was really horrified at the thought. Even the sweet image of Alice Bain could not drive from my mind the fearful concomitants of my love. I felt as guilty as a murderer. I was almost the betrayer of Cousin Lou; the violater of the most sacred traditions of my family. Besides, there was their sure anger. No one could say to what length it might go. I was not afraid, but I knew that the hatred of all the De Jeunettes was not a thing to be lightly incurred. At times I even thought of buying my future peace by killing the memory of the new love and marrying the old one. So a year crept on and I knew not what I should do. I could not tell my own mind. To drown what had come to be a real trouble, I had devoted myself to my profession, had gambled not a little, and had drank more than beseemed a De Jeunette outside his own house. The son of my law tutor, a young man of my own age, drank much and played heavily. I had become his security for several debts contracted, as I believed, at the gambling table; I knew their amount was considerable, but could not tell how much. It mattered little, as I had no fear but he would redeem them.

No one suspected my folly. All observed my altered demeanor, but attributed it to other causes. The people said I was not so proud as my family, and wanted to be popular. The De Jeunettes said my profession had turned my head and made me forget my kindred. They began to rally me about Cousin Lou, and ask when I was going to marry and settle down as a De Jeunette should. I put them off as best I could, and grew more and more reserved—more and more estranged from my family. I went but seldom to any of the home-sites that were the pride of our family. Queen Louie began to droop. I could see it. Her eyes sought mine with a sad, pleading expression when we met. I knew that she was repining at my neglect. I despised myself for my folly, and yet persisted in it.

I went to the river-place—"The Cedars," we called it—several times during that year for a day or two, once or twice for a week. Of course, I saw Alice Bain at such times, for she was an orphan, and lived with her uncle, the overseer. Each sight of her increased my enthralment. No one suspected it, because I was a De Jeunette and she only the niece of an overseer. Her manner to me was that of the most simple, modest, and engaging frankness.

At length I came down to the plantation just as the spring freshet set in. The next morning the river was too high to cross, and I was imprisoned at The Cedars until the waters should subside. For two days it rained continuously, and on the evening of the third, just as the sun was going down, the clouds broke away, revealing in his setting glow almost as wide a waste of waters as greeted the eye of the patriarch when he looked forth from the unsettled ark. The overseer had been busy on the bottoms, saving fences and strengthening dikes and water-gaps, with the whole force of the plantation. He came in to his supper late that night, and I remarked to him that he could rest now, as the rain was over.

"Yes, Mr. De Jeunette," he answered, "the rain is over, but the water keeps running and the river is still rising. If it keeps on at this rate till midnight, I 'calculate it will come up to the Great Fresh of 'Ninety-Five. I was looking at the marks my father cut on a water-oak at the mouth of the branch above the ford to mark that rise, just at daylight-down, and it was getting within a few feet of it then."

"Are you going out again to-night, uncle?" asked his niece.

"Yes, Allie," he answered, as he lighted his pipe and put on his hat. "While the up-country is full of water and the river rising, there is no knowing what mischief it may not do."

The full moon was casting her peaceful radiance over the watery scene, obscured only now and then by light fleecy clouds that blew across her disk. Alice approached the window and looked out.

"What a splendid night!" she exclaimed. "Did you ever see a 'fresh' by moonlight, Mr. Charles?" she asked, turning to me excitedly.

I admitted that I had not.

"Oh, it is grand!" said she. "I used to watch it often when I was a child, and sometimes do so now, when I can get uncle to go with me. Won't you go to-night?" she asked coaxingly, as she went up to the old man and clasped her hands caressingly about his arm.

"No, dear, I can't. The hands is nigh worn out, and if there's nobody to look after them, a heap of truck may be lost that might be saved

with a little care. But as you say, it will be a
sight worth seein' with such a moon lightin' up
the roarin' flood, that rushes on as if it was alive
an' strivin' to win a race, risin' like a ridge in the
centre and drawing everything that it clutches
along the banks to the middle. Did you ever
know that, Mr. Charles? It's a hungry, ravenous
thing, is a river on a rise. Trees and rails and
fodder-stacks and bridges, whatever it gets hold
on, it rushes to the middle, and puts a guard of
mad, sullen, treacherous, still water, full of back-
sets and eddies, atween it and the shore. It's a
hard thing to tussle with, is a mad river. It don't
let up and come again, like the sea, but keeps its
hold, and sucks and grips every minute, gatherin'
sometimes into a whirl and then rushin' on as if
dead certain of its prey, and mockin' at his despair.
A cruel, treacherous thing, Mr. De Jeunette, is a
big fresh!"

"Well done, uncle!" cried Alice, clapping her
hands and laughing at the enthusiasm of the old
man's description.

"There, there, gal. Don't laugh at me. I
know I cannot do it justice, but I'll tell ye, Mr.
Charles, if I was a painter—not to say a poet—I
wouldn't rest, I *couldn't* rest, till I'd put such a

fresh as this on paper, or canvas, or whatever it is
they use for such things."

I could see his eye flash and his thin nostril and
lip quiver as he went out.   There was good blood
in the hard-headed old Scotch-descended overseer, if he was poor.

He stopped for a moment on the porch, and
then came back and opened the door of the room
where we were.

"O Allie!" he said.   "If you want to go down
to the Pint, perhaps Mr. Charles will ride with
you?"

He looked inquiringly in my direction, and I
assented with an eagerness which I feared might
be observed, but the freshet itself was too exciting
for any excess of emotion on my part to be noticed.

"Very well," said he, "I will order the horses
to be brought around.   You must be right careful
of her, Mr. Charles.   She's a mighty venturesome
little thing.   She knows every foot of the ground,
though, and there can't be no danger unless she
rides smack into the river itself.   There ain't nary
cross-cut nor set-back that comes nigh the path."

CHAPTER IV.

IT was a glorious night. There was little mud, as the rain had fallen with such force that the road was packed, and only the surface water splashed about us, sparkling in the moonlight, as we galloped towards the Point which lay a mile or more below. The Cedars was a wedge of land that lay between two rivers of almost equal volume. The Point was the extremity below which they met and formed a single stream. We could hear the sullen roar of each sounding across the narrow neck, like an angry challenge to the other, as we rode along.

A short distance from the house the road left the high lands and went down upon the second bottoms, an alluvial plateau some feet above the first bottoms which were now covered by the swollen flood. These second bottoms had undoubtedly, in some former age, been to .the streams they separated what the first bottoms, or actual low grounds, were now, and had been subject to overflow for a long period, though the river had never been over them since the settlement of the country.

At the extreme end of the Point the confluent currents had deposited the sediment and drift with which they were charged in past ages, until there had been built up a gravelly mound considerably above the level of the second bottoms which we had traversed.

Arriving at this, we dismounted and I picketed the horses, after which we scrambled over the rough surface to the extreme end of the Point. It was indeed a strange, wild scene. I did not wonder that it had taken such a hold upon the old overseer, still less that it quite enchanted my impressible companion.

The stream upon the right was black and sullen, and seemed to be gliding onward with a silent, stealthy purpose of revenge. The one upon the left, less in volume, was a more boisterous and impetuous torrent. It was of yellowish red by day, as if it flowed through banks of ochre, but in the moonlight it showed a soft creamy white. Below the Point the two streams met, only to pursue each its way side by side with the other, but unmingled, unmerged; so that below us ran a river with its right bank bathed in darkness and its left a gleaming band of light.

"An evident misjoinder," I said lightly, as I came to the extreme verge of the Point, almost over the mad whirlpool which their junction made, and stood beside Alice Bain looking out on the strange scene, "like an ill-assorted marriage."

"And no wonder," she answered quickly, "when we look at the means which caused their union." She pointed to a low, dark-looking range of hills that lay to the left. "That," she continued, "is the end of the water-shed between the Saxipahaw and the Neuse. The Indians had a tradition about these streams, as I have heard, which is really poetical. They say that long ago, when the earth was young, the Saxipahaw started in the hill country and ran a long way to the eastward, or perhaps north-eastward, trying to mate with the Laughing Water—the Dan; but that ungallant fellow ran away from her, and then she came sedately along through the Haw fields, half mourning a first love, but soon conceived the hope of uniting with the Neuse. But the Manitou placed the Okoneechee Hills across her way, and turned her course sharp to the south-eastward, along a rough and rugged channel. Then she

came on here, black and sullen, only to become
the unwilling bride of the .impetuous river which
rushes on her like a wild beast on its prey."

We stood leaning against the solitary pine
which had sprung from the mound of *débris*, and
held its place doubtfully over the hissing, hungry
flood, I on its right and in the shadow, she on
the left, bathed in moonlight—the rugged bole
between.

"You are of Scotch descent, Miss Alice?" I
said inquiringly, at length.

"Yes," she answered, "on my father's side.
My mother was English, I have heard him say.
She died when I was very young"—

"And I am of French extraction—old Huguenot," I said musingly, and was silent again.

"What could put any such speculation in your
mind at this time, Mr. De Jeunette?" she asked
at length, curiously.

There was not a quaver in her tone to denote a
suspicion of the wild passion which was raging in
my breast. She was all womanly grace and can-
dor. I glanced down upon her as she stood at
my left, with the full summer moon lighting her
slight form and tingeing her many-hued locks
with mellow light, while I, dark and swart as my

fiery ancestors, was half hidden in the shadow of the pine.

Love was triumphant. I could hesitate no longer, so I answered meaningly, "The river."

"The river! How should the river suggest such inquiry?" she asked.

"Do you not see," I answered, pointing to the united waters before us, "that the right is dark and the left bright "—

"And so," she began—

"So," I interrupted, "with Covenanter and Huguenot—bright Scotch and swart Norman."

She was so innocent she only thought it a gallant jest on my part, and answered without a moment's hesitation.

"But you said yourself," she laughed, "that it was an ill-assorted union—a most evil omen to be thus applied."

"Nay, nay," I rejoined, "that is only an appearance. You know that when the two rivers have once united they become placid and peaceful in their onward course, and the smiling current which sinks into the ocean is so bright and lovely that it was named by its first discoverers 'The Fair'—'Cape Fair,' which later generations have corrupted into 'Fear.'"

"But that was only the result of a philosophy which made the best of a bad bargain. The rivers united because the mountains stood across their chosen paths," she answered as lightly as before.

"How if they had united in spite of mountains that stood between?" I asked eagerly.

"What do you mean, Mr. De Jeunette?" she exclaimed, with a start, and flashed up at me a look of surprised inquiry.

I had leaned forward, and the moon shone full upon my face, revealing its excited workings.

"I mean that no mountain could keep me from coming to you, Alice Bain," I replied, in a voice as hoarse as the roar of the mad river.

She started with an exclamation of overwhelming surprise, and half turned from me. As she did so her eye fell upon the moonlit stream, and she exclaimed, with a start:

"See, see, Mr. De Jeunette, how the river has risen! It is above Lewis's rock!" And she pointed to where I had seen a huge boulder rising above the surface when we first came to the Point. Her voice was tremulous with excitement and alarm as she proceeded:

"Oh, what an awful freshet! The high water

of 'Ninety-five did not overflow that at all. That
was why it was named Lewis's rock. He was
washed away and caught on that, and stayed two
days and nights till he was taken off in a canoe!"
She had not thought of love, and the sight of the
stream at such unusual height drove my avowal
from her mind. "And it is still rising," she continued. "Do you not see how it arches in the
middle? It is always so in a fresh. When it
begins to fall it will be the lowest there. See the
eddies along the current! I never saw them so
thick—and—look there, Mr. De Jeunette?" She
pointed to the stream below where we stood.
The restless, eager waters were lapping and pat-
tering among the loose stones and driftwood
almost at our feet.

"What is that?" said Alice suddenly. I had
heard it once or twice before, but had not thought
anything of it. It was the sharp, anxious neigh
of my horse Sachem. Now that I listened to it
I noted an unmistakable accent, so to speak, of
alarm and terror in his familiar call.

I comprehended the situation in an instant.
The river had risen, and the low-lying second bottoms had been overflowed.

"We must go back, Miss Alice. The river has

burst across the Point, I fear, and we have not a moment to lose!"

"It cannot be!" she answered, in that tone in which persons argue against indisputable but unpleasant facts. "The Point land never overflows!"

"But you forget, Miss Alice, that you just said that the river was higher than it was in 'Ninety-five, which is the highest that has ever been known here."

"Oh, it cannot be!" she cried, as we scrambled over the loose rocks and low bushes towards the horses.

Before we came to them we met what we dreaded—the insidious, silent enemy, creeping among the leaves and stones, with a half-gurgling laugh.

"Stay here, Miss Alice!" I cried. "I will get the horses. Do not be afraid," I cried lightly; "it will be all right, and an adventure we shall have great sport over, some day."

"Oh, you do not know!" she cried, as she turned towards me a face pallid with fear. "You do not know the terrible, treacherous river! It has swept across the Point, as you say, and who can tell where the current is now, or find the road!"

I raised her in my arms, and placed her on a rock where she could sit down. How my heart beat! I was glad of this terrible danger. I almost hoped we might die there together. I would tell her how I loved her and we would sleep in the grave together, and Cousin Louie should never know my secret. But the poor child's terror was so extreme that I would not breathe a word of my mad thoughts to her. I made her sit down on the rock to which I had carried her, talking all the time in light, cheery tones, caught one kiss from her upturned, quivering lips, which were all unconscious of the larceny, and dashed away into the water to Sachem, who was now calling to me in evident terror.

It was but a few yards, yet it seemed miles through the deepening waters. The horses were tethered just on the outskirts of a growth of stunted oaks on the little rise which constituted the Point. When I reached them the water had risen to the girth, and Sachem was pawing the creeping thing and snorting furiously. He recognized me in an instant, and became as quiet as a lamb.

He was a compact and powerful thoroughbred, and had been a favorite from a suckling. He was of a stock noted for endurance and sagacity. As soon as I came his excitement vanished. He occasionally raised his head and looked over the watery waste (which was all around us now) with a snort of inquiry, but was obedient to my lightest word. Even in the midst of the danger that threatened, I was proud of my noble steed. I patted his arched neck, and called him pet names as I unloosed the bridle with a sort of delirious joy.

The mare which my companion had ridden had not the high breeding of my noble bay. She was cold-blooded, and shrunk and cowered among the low bushes, pulling wildly at the halter, and gazing with swelling nostrils and rolling eyes at the wild torrent that now rushed between us and the upland. Neither words nor blows could soothe or subdue her. She was thoroughly and uncontrollably terrified. The instinct of self-preservation had overridden the training of man, and she had gone back to the wildness of her base ancestry upon the banks of our eastern shore.

I hastily stripped the saddle from her back, and bound it upon Sachem, and, taking his upon my arm, made my way back to Alice Bain. My mind was made up. I was sure the mare would never

take the water, and equally sure that Sachem
would bear Alice safely home. If, then, the
water subsided before it reached my perch—well.
If not, there would be one less De Jeunette and
no cousin Lou to upbraid me for inconstancy.

I lifted Alice into the saddle and put her foot
into the stirrup, without a word. Then I gave
her the reins in one hand and a lock of Sachem's
long silky mane in the other.

"Miss Alice," I said—huskily, I do not doubt
—"do not try to guide him. Let him have his
head and just cling to your seat, and he will take
you home."

Poor child! she had not noticed what I had
done before.

"O Mr. De Jeunette!" she cried, "how could
you give me your horse? Dare you trust my
poor filly?"

"I shall not think of it," I replied. "She is
past all control with fear."

As I spoke, the mare broke from her fasten-
ings, and rushed wildly past us. I caught the
shawl from Alice's shoulders and threw it over
Sachem's head, that he might not see the course
she took. Struggling through the rising water
and thick bushes, the terrified beast rushed across

the now narrow island, and dashed into the resistless torrent beyond. We watched her silently, as
she swam with the stream until her head was lost
in the distance and darkness.

Then I unmuffled Sachem's head, and began
leading him away from the pine. This was the
only landmark on which I could rely. I went on
and on until the water was above my hips, and
surging past me like a mill-race. I could be of no
further use to her, and I knew that the strong
high-bred horse would take her safely across. I
stopped and said:

"Good-by, Miss Alice. Remember. Do not try
to guide him. He is of good Pilot stock, and can
be trusted. When you get across, call as loudly
as you can, that I may know that you are safe."

"But what will you do?"

"The best I can. No matter—only—. Put
your head down lower, so that I can whisper in
your ear. There now, little Allie, remember—
remember always — my last message. Do you
hear me?"

"Yes, Mr. De Jeunette," tearfully.

"And will you remember it very carefully?"

"As long as I live," came solemnly from the
trembling lips.

"Remember, then, that Charles De Jeunette loves Alice Bain better than all the world beside."

A startled moan burst from her as she half fell upon my neck. I held her close for an instant, and then said:

"Give me one kiss, Allie, darling."

"Our lips met for an instant. Then I placed her well in the saddle again and loosed the horse, who was growing restive.

"Do not forget to call when you reach the land," I cried, as she rode away. There was no answer, and I struggled back towards the pine which marked the highest ground, uncertain whether she had heard my injunction or not.

I found the island rapidly decreasing in size. The water was rising still. The rock on which I had placed Alice was just above water. I scrambled to it and looked out over the waste to see, if I could, what had become of the horse and his rider. I could see nothing of them. I waited patiently. The water crept over the rock. I looked and listened. If I could but know that Alice was safe—I cared little for myself. At length I thought I heard a faint hail, and answered it with a long hulloo—the *Hea-yi-bee!* of the piney-woods hunters. I was not sure, but I

thought a woman's voice replied. Then I heard
a loud, questioning neigh. It was Sachem's call
for his master. I knew it well. The water was
above my knees. I looked around and saw that
the pine was gone. The fierce current was rapidly
washing away the loose soil of the Point. Again
I heard the neigh of my faithful horse. A
thought struck me. I put my hands to my
mouth and sent a shrill, piercing whistle across
the water. I had been used to call him in that
way. No ordinary object would, I knew, prevent
his coming to me if he heard it. Whether he
would take the water again I did not know. Alice
was safe. The rest mattered little.

Yes, he hears me! the long answering neigh
comes across the turgid expanse. Words could
not say plainer "What shall I do?" than the neigh
of my noble steed. Again I sound the call. There
is a hurried whinny and I hear no more. Again
and again I call, but there is no response. Has
he taken the water or has Alice ridden him away
to get help for me? The water is still creeping
higher. I take off my boots and remove my
clothing by degrees, still whistling occasionally to
guide Sachem should he be returning. The time
grows long. He will not come. I whistle once

more. There is a smothered whinny from the water not a dozen yards away.

" Here, here, Sachem, my brave horse !" And now I pat his nose and see the white spume fly from his nostrils.

Taking a good grip in his mane I turn his head, and swimming beside him, we make for the shore. Before we reach the upland, it is alive with torches, and friendly arms grasp us both as we touch bottom.

CHAPTER V.

A BETROTHAL.

I DID not see Alice until the next morning.
They told me how the noble horse had
brought her safely through the rushing torrent,
and when he answered my whistle with a neigh,
she had stripped the saddle from him and sent
him back to me, while she ran on to the house to
give the alarm.

"She was mighty took back, too," said her
uncle, "to think she had ridden away your horse
and left you there to drown alone. Poor gal!
she been taking on powerful about it ever since;
and it was all her aunt could do to keep her from
coming back with us, wet as she was, and knowin' she could do no good. Here, you boys, some
of you, go on ahead and tell Miss Alice that Mr.
De Jeunette is all right," he said to the negroes
who were with us.

It was a useless command, for a dozen had
already flown to the overseer's house with the

news, which they knew would win her smiles and thanks.

The next morning, when I went down to breakfast, the overseer was sitting on the porch looking off upon the landscape glistening in the sunlight of a cloudless morning. The river had reached its highest some time during the night, he said, and he could now rest from the exciting labors of the past few days. He would go around in the evening and see that "the suck," which always sets in when the fresh begins to fall, did as little damage as might be.

While he spoke Alice appeared. I can see her yet as she stood in the low doorway, the light muslin falling daintily about her slight form, her face still flushed with the ebb of last night's excitement, and her eyes full of soft light, which spoke of tears that were not all bitterness.

In the first glance I read her heart. Her face flushed in an instant, and coming forward she gave me her hand, saying, as her eyes fell beneath my glances:

"O Mr. De Jeunette, I am so ashamed that I came away last night without even—"

"Without even answering my question?" I

interrupted. "Never mind. I would much rather you would do so now."

She looked up almost appealingly, her face flaming like the morning she adorned, but did not remove her hand from mine.

I put my arm about her waist, drew her to me, and kissed her lips. She hid her face upon my breast with a half-frightened sob, and I stroked the sunny ringlets that fell about the shapely head, while the morning sun played amid their lights and shadows.

The overseer had watched this by-play with amazement, which he could not read aright. He had arisen and came towards us with a look on his face scarcely removed from horror.

"Poor gal!" he said in a pitying tone, as he laid his hand upon her arm. "Last night was too much for her to bear. She's always been delicate like, and I 'spects she's hystericky now."

"Will you let me have her, Mr. Bain?" I asked as I kept on stroking the fair head that nestled closer at my words.

"What! what! you do not mean"—said the old man in an amazement, which stopped short at this point for want of words to express its intensity.

"I mean," I said, "to ask you for your niece, Alice Bain, to be my wife."

A low cry of joy came from the head on my breast. I bowed, and kissed its golden covering.

The old man tottered backward to his chair.

"You—you do not mean it. You cannot mean it!" he exclaimed, and then added angrily, as another thought came over him, "You are trifling with my little gal, sir!"

"As God is my judge, Mr. Bain, I have no other hope in this world," I answered solemnly.

He sat down and gazed at us in unsatisfied wonder. A climbing rose ran over the post of the piazza near which we stood, and I plucked the fresh storm-washed blossoms, and put them in Allie's hair.

"O Mistress, Mistress!" said the overseer, calling to his wife.

"Well," she answered, and a portly dame stood in the doorway, cheerful and smiling.

"Mistress, Mr. Charles wants our Allie."

"*Wants* her!" returned the dame with a laugh. "Hasn't he got her?"

The laugh was a corrective. It infected the entire group. I laughed so that I deranged the roses in Alice's hair. A little ripple came up from my breast. Even the overseer could not help chuckling dryly at the unexpected reply.

" But he wants to marry her !" he said.

" To marry her ?" The ripple of laughter faded from her fair matronly face as she looked earnestly toward us.

" That is my wish," I said, answering her look rather than her words.

" Then I don't see why you shouldn't," she said thoughtfully.

" But he is a De Jeunette, wife ! A De Jeunette, Mistress !" said the old man excitedly.

" And if he was a king, Alec, he is none too good for our little Alice !" answered his wife, turning sharply upon him.

" True,—true," said the old man doubtfully; " if he means it—"

" Did a De Jeunette ever lie ?" I said to him hotly.

" No, no. But it is so strange—so sudden, Mr. Charles. I'm powerful 'fraid this 'll be an unfortunate fresh to us, Mistress."

The old woman went up to him and put her hand on his almost bare crown lovingly, as she said :

" We have done our duty, Alec. If Allie is willing, why should we stand in the way ?"

"Oh! I don't mean to object," he returned, absently—" only it is so strange—so sudden—so unreasonable-like !"

" Then, little Allie," I said gayly, " it is for you to decide. What do you say? Will you marry a terrible De Jeunette ?"

She raised her head and looked up with her eyes full of lovelight ; and there under the dewy rose-spray in the bright morning sunlight I kissed my rose-crowned queen.

This was our courtship. She begged for a year's delay to our marriage, that she might fit herself still better for the terrible station to which my love, as she thought, had raised her. The next morning I went home, and within a week Alice had gone to attend a famous school at the North. It was not necessary, for the old over- seer had given her every advantage, and few of the aristocratic De Jeunette clique could boast of as thorough culture as my little woodland bird.

It was agreed, however, that our engagement should be kept secret until the year had passed.

CHAPTER VI.

MOTHER AND SON.

MY cousin Louie was a favorite with my mother, who had become almost as much of a De Jeunette as if the blood of the Vaudois, instead of that of the most bigoted of papistical stock, ran in her veins. It seemed as if no one could be submitted to the charm of our De Jeunette life—proud, haughty, and exclusive, yet cordial and tender to each other—without yielding to its influences, and, if allied to the family at all, counting that the proudest quartering in the field of his descent. So, though my mother often accounted for my eccentricities by calling me "her Neal," she was far more desirous that I should be a De Jeunette, and was chiefly proud that she had borne a De Jeunette, for I was an only child.

Scarcely had Alice gone away when my trouble commenced. I had assured her that all I had to do to secure her proper reception as my wife, was to announce the fact to my family. Such I half thought to be the truth. I intended to carry it through with a high hand, as I had all previous innovations which I had chosen to attempt. Alas! I sadly mistook the imperious nature of the stock from which I came.

My mother had been an invalid for a year or two. I do not know of what disease she was ailing. She had not seemed very ill, and I knew had not been considered "dangerous."

One evening a boy came to my office with a led horse, and a request from my mother that I would ride to Beaumont without delay. She did not say she was worse, and the boy—one of the home-servants—thought "Miss Mary was much the same as usual." I was very busy that afternoon preparing an important case. No matter. The instinct of the De Jeunette was strong in my breast—stronger than I knew, or would allow— and no De Jeunette of whatever age had ever failed to answer and obey the request of his mother. That was a sacred and immemorial tradition in our family. I was a De Jeunette, and in twenty minutes my client had been dismissed with instructions to come at a more convenient season, my office door was locked, and I was on my way to Beaumont.

I found my mother in a state of strange excitement. She was sitting propped up in her bed,
paler and weaker than I had ever seen her before,
but with a recurrent flush upon her delicate
cheek, and a peculiar light in her warm gray eye
which I had never witnessed before. Louie was
with her, attending upon and caring for her. That
magnificent beauty which had given her the
sobriquet of Queen in all the country round
seemed to be enhanced by the contrast with the
pale blond invalid whose charms neither years
nor disease could altogether obliterate. There
was a look of unwonted tenderness, too, in the
grand dark eyes as she looked up at me when I
entered the room. She was standing with her
left arm thrown carelessly over the mass of pillows against which my mother reclined, upon the
high, old-fashioned, four-poster bed. With her
right hand she was fanning her charge, while from
a small round table beside the bed came up the
mingled fragrance of mignonette and the spicy
honeysuckle, which grows far more luxuriant
among our Carolina hills than in its Oriental home.
It was a favorite with Louie, and in its season,
which is almost the whole summer, its dull-green
leaves and delicate waxy-white blossoms were

always to be found at her throat, in her girdle, or twined among the meshes of her abundant hair. And in truth its strong, subtle, pungent odor, as well as the flowers and leaves, admirably became the passionate intensity and unobtrusive self-reliance of my cousin. She was dressed that day, I remember, in pure white, relieved only by the foliage of this flower.

As I rose up after saluting my mother, who was still clasping my right hand in her two feeble ones, I gave my left to Louie, and, leaning forward, kissed her lips. It was no new thing. I had kissed my beautiful cousin almost as often as we had met since we were children together. But there seemed to be some new meaning in this salutation, both for her and for me. It was long since I had seen her; I was dazzled with her beauty and confused with the sense of my new secret. If she spoke at all I have forgotten it. I suppose she did, and I may have answered mechanically.

What first impressed my consciousness was that she had dropped my hand and was going from the room. Her cheek and neck, even the delicate ears, were flushed a burning crimson.

I felt my mother stroking my hand with hers.

I looked down and saw her face radiant with a peaceful joy.

" Is she not glorious ?" she whispered, her eyes following the retreating figure to the door.

"Divine !" I murmured absently, but without hesitation.

"You are right," she responded, "for Louie is more noble in mind and spirit than beautiful in face and form. Go, my son," she continued, releasing my hand, "and make her yours at once. Her heart is yearning to bestow its sweets, and half-grieved at your ungallant coldness toward her. Go, and let me see those whom I most love united before I die."

I stood thunderstruck. The fond hope of my mother and the glorious vision of Louie's beauty strove in my excited mind with the memory of my absent Alice. How dim that memory seemed ! How foreign from Beaumont and its luxurious accompaniments ! Had I been foolish to pluck that wildwoods flower ? God forgive me if I thought so for one moment.

"Go, my son," urged my mother. "Do not be afraid to meet your fate. Trust me ; Louie has been waiting to say 'Yes' this many a day," she added with a smile.

She thought it was fear of a refusal that fettered my feet. At once my trouble of mind was gone. It was as if Alice stood beside me and strengthened me by her presence. It was a terrible task that lay before me, but I would not shrink from it. I sat down upon the edge of my mother's bed and took her hand again.

"Mother," I said, earnestly and tenderly, for I feared to wound that loving heart as I knew I must. "Mother, I cannot do it!"

"Cannot do what?" she asked, in surprise, "Cannot ask your cousin Louie to be your wife? Why, when became my boy so timid?"

"It is not timidity, mother."

"Not timidity? What then is it?" Then, looking into my troubled face, she continued half banteringly, "Perhaps you who have so nearly cast off your relatives do not consider the Queen of the De Jeunettes good enough to mate with you?"

Her sarcasm had a double sting.

"O mother!" I said hurriedly, "you know I never had such a thought. The truth is—I—I—"

"Well, 'You'—what! Foolish boy!" Still smiling, and unconscious of the terrible bolt which was soon to blast her love and confidence. "You have been a bachelor hermit so long that you have lost your share of sense, very nearly."

"But, mother."

"Well, I hear."

"I am already—engaged."

"What!" exclaimed my mother, her countenance becoming at once of a dull ashen hue, with astonishment and horror. "Engaged! Engaged —and without my knowledge! Oh, how could you?"

"It was mere accident," I hastened to say; "I had no idea—"

"Of course not," she interrupted hotly, "you had no idea that it would make any difference whether your family were suited with your action or not!"

"I did not mean that, mother," I replied. "I intended to say that I had no intention of acting contrary to your wishes, but I was, in a measure, the victim of circumstances."

"Oh, if it is only that," she said, with evident relief, "it can all be settled without any such sacrifice. You have undoubtedly been the victim of some designing thing, and—"

"But, mother," I said, now doubly embarrassed, "you will not understand me. Whatever you

may think of me, I have never disgraced my manhood, however much the pride of my family may
have suffered from my acts."

"Pray then, if it is not asking too much, will
you explain what you did mean?" she said
coldly.

"I meant that circumstances had conspired to
deprive me of all volition in the matter before I
could consult with you, or I certainly should have
done so before taking such a step," I answered.

"I do not understand how that could be. Explain !"

"I became enamored of the lady whom I expect to marry, and declared my love when I was
so situated that I had little hope of ever seeing
you again," I said.

"You choose to speak in riddles, sir," she said
sneeringly. "Perhaps you are not willing to reveal the name of this paragon who so overshad-
ows the Queen of the De Jeunettes! Some low-
down thing your family would never dream of
recognizing, I presume."

My face was hot. I could not hear my sweet
Alice insulted, even by my mother.

"She is one," I said quickly, "whom any family
might be proud to own."

"Name her, if you please, sir; name her, and do not give me your opinion!"

I hesitated. How should I tell that proud and exclusive woman, the mother whose strong, fierce love was centred upon me and my well-being, but to whose mind poverty was a sin, and whose ideas of caste were as exclusive as those of a Brahmin—how should I tell her that the bride I had chosen was the penniless Alice Bain, the niece of an overseer!

"I must acknowledge she is not wealthy," I began.

"Her name, her name!" she said fiercely.

"But she is of a good, respectable family, and—',

"Oh, I smell the shop," she said impatiently. "Name her, and be done with it. Don't drag up the filthy concomitants!"

"Alice Bain," I said shortly.

"Alice Bain? Alice Bain? A pretty name enough," said my mother, in some surprise; "but who is she? Where does she live?"

"On the river."

"On the river. That *is* definite! And, pray, how long is the river, and in what part of its course does she live, sir?" she asked, with the cold, hard sneer again.

"Near the Ford—Quelloe's Ford," I answered.

" Near your father's Point Plantation?"

" On it," I responded.

"On it!—on it! On your father's Point Plantation!"

" Yes, at The Cedars."

" At The Cedars? How can that be? Who *is* she, Charles?"

" She is the niece of Alexander Bain, my father's overseer."

"The niece of your father's overseer! My God, Charles, could you not be content with any less disgrace to the family? But you shall never marry the jade! Never, sir!"

" Mother,—"

" Don't call me mother! I disown you from this moment, unless you renounce her at once!"

" I cannot do it."

"You mean you will not!"

"Well, then, I *will* not."

" That is right! Complete your work. You have disgraced your family now. O Charles! Charles!" she cried, with a wail of agony which struck to my heart, "how have I loved you, and stood by you, and defended you from your father's anger, and against the aspersions of your

enemies! And now, O God! you will marry an
overseer's brat! The spawn of a man who sells
himself to whip your father's niggers! O my
God! If only you had died, or I, before my heart
was broken with this disgrace!"

"But, mother," I said, trying to soften her
anger.

"Stop, sir! not a word. Hear what I have to
say. Either break off this horrible misalliance, or
never come into my presence again, living or
dead! Never enter this house, never speak my
name, nor call yourself my son, for I will disown
you before all the world. Stop! do not answer
now! Hand me my watch!"

I took it from the table and put it in her hand.

"Now go," she said, "and sit in the window
yonder. I will call you in half an hour and hear
your answer. Go now!"

I started towards the embrasure. My mind
was already made up, but I longed for a moment
of time as one does when condemned to die, in
the vain hope that something—I knew not what
—might happen, to modify the terrible wrath of
my mother. I had never in all my life seen her
angry before. I think few ever had. Hers was
one of those natures which are seldom wrought

into a passion, and whose anger when once stirred is like the besom of destruction, sweeping all before it. It was so terrible that it almost stunned me. I could not comprehend it. Though I had no idea of yielding to it, yet it terrified me to the core, and distressed me unspeakably. I would go and see if I could not devise some means to allay it.

I had hardly taken three steps when my mother called me by name. I turned. She had started from her pillows and was gazing at me with a wild yearning look, her arms outstretched towards me in mute entreaty. I sprang towards her and caught her in my arms. Her head fell upon my breast, and a torrent of wild sobs and tears, intermixed with ejaculations of grief and entreaty, burst from her. After a time she became calmer and again directed me to go. As I turned to obey, she caught me again.

"Once more, one more embrace," she said, as she kissed me again and again. "O Charles! remember that your poor mother begs and prays you to grant her this one last request! She will never make another, Charles—and she has not been exacting—not of you, my boy, has she? Remember her life is in your answer. Go now—go—go!" and she pushed me from her.

I went again to the embrasure of the window
and looked off towards the other seats of the
family, for a moment, trying to devise something
which I might say to appease this fond woman—
this mother whom I loved, as I verily believe I
did at that moment, better than all else on earth,
even Alice Bain. Yet I had no idea of renouncing
Alice. I do not think it was so much the strength
of my love as the stubbornness of my character,
the dread I had of yielding, and the conviction
that my mother's request was unjust and required
a shameful and dishonorable act on my part.

It was perhaps five or ten minutes, when my
mother called me, and I returned to her bedside.
She was leaning forward with flushed cheeks and
eager, burning eyes.

"You have decided?" she asked tremblingly.

I merely bowed.

"And you will—you will renounce that woman.
You will do as your mother begs you to do?" she
asked.

"Mother, it is unreasonable—and—"

"Yes or No? We have had argument enough!"
she interrupted. "For the last time, will you give
up this overseer's brat?"

"I can not," I answered firmly.

" What? What ?" she said confusedly.

" I can not do it," I repeated.

Her countenance changed in an instant. Instead of love and anxiety, only pride and fierce, white-heat anger were there."

" Then go !" she cried. " Go ! you are no longer my son !"

She gave a slight cough, and a red stream burst over her thin lips. I sprang to her. She waved me back with a look of aversion on her face, and pointed to the bell on the stand by her bed. I touched it hurriedly, and my cousin Louie came in. She glanced from one to the other inquiringly as she advanced. Seeing the condition of my mother, she became at once the skillful and collected nurse, wiped away the blood, gave her some soothing draught, and was preparing to lay her back upon her pillows, when she spoke slowly and with evident difficulty, pointing her thin white finger towards me :

"Send him out of the house, Louie. He is not my son, nor your cousin." In answer to her inquiring look, "You may give him your congratulations, though. He is about to marry—*marry*—the niece of his father's overseer!"

Louie flashed up at me a look of surprise, and

then turned again to my mother, as if doubting her sanity.

"Oh, it is true, Louie! He will not deny it!"

The look of inquiry changed into magnificent scorn on Louie's face, as she saw it was no invention of delirium that was being told to her.

"Congratulate him, Louie, and send him away; and, Louie, see to it that he never looks upon my face again, alive or dead."

"But, mother," I said protestingly.

"Go away! go away!" she cried hoarsely, but fiercely, with wild gestures of aversion.

"Go!" cried Louie. "Do you not see that you are killing her!"

I mounted my horse and rode away from Beaumont. The next day I was formally notified by my father that I had been disinherited, both by himself and by my mother as regarded the property in her own right, and that the entire estate would be devised to Cousin Louie in my stead, and that I should receive no benefit therefrom except by marriage with the heiress. I was also notified that the family would hold no intercourse with me, and that if I came upon the premises I would be arrested as a common trespasser. In a day or two the county was flooded with circulars stating the fact of my disinheritance, and warning all persons not to credit me on the strength and faith of the De Jeunette name or estate, as none wearing it would be responsible for my indebtedness.

CHAPTER VII.

MOVEMENT.

IN a few days my mother died, never having recovered from the excitement of that last interview with me. I learned from the servants— for the family strictly maintained the embargo which had been laid upon me—that my father railed upon me as a murderer, and threatened me with violence should I attempt to attend the burial of my mother. Nevertheless I went. I knew that my father and the entire family were fierce and violent when their passions were aroused, but I was too much like them to be deterred by any threats they might make.

The service had begun when I reached Beaumont. At the door I was met by an old servant, who entreated me not to enter. I pushed by him and went in and sat down near the coffin. There was a large assembly of friends and neighbors. Two events always broke down the exclusiveness of the De Jeunettes—the marriage of a young member of the family and the death of an old one. Every one, rich and poor, high and low, was invited to come and rejoice with them on the one occasion, and came freely to mourn with them on the other. So there was a large assemblage in the house. It seemed to me that every face was black with wrath. When the services were over, and the undertaker came forward to open the coffin for a last look at the dead, my father arose, put his hand on the man's arm and whispered a word in his ear. The man seemed surprised, but answered nothing. The pall-bearers, at a gesture from him, took up the coffin and moved towards the door. We went out to the family burying-ground, and the gentle, loving, long-suffering, but proud and inflexible mother, whom my unfortunate idiosyncrasies had wounded to death, was laid to rest. Her last request had been fulfilled. I was not permitted to look upon her face after she had sent me from her with that cold, repellent stare, her features pallid as marble, and her lips crimson with the blood which had burst forth in consequence of her excitement. Was I her murderer? I stood leaning against a tree near the grave pondering this question till all had gone.

No one had spoken to me. In the midst of my

own, I was alone. All looked upon me as a leper. Whatever I might think, whatever might be the truth, every De Jeunette counted me the murderer, the cold, deliberate, unfeeling murderer, of the most charming woman in the connection. Not only this: the general sentiment agreed with this family feeling. The De Jeunettes were close-mouthed. They did not talk of their affairs. In joy or sorrow they were the same to the world. They did not conceal their wrath towards me, but they gave no reason for it other than that I had caused my mother's death. I could give none; so the world accepted as a fact the statement that I had killed my mother by some act of wanton disobedience.

A servant approached and put into my hand a mourning card, with these words hastily written on it:

"Leave Beaumont *at once*. Meet me at the old church to-night at ten o'clock! Do not delay!　　　　　　　　　　　　　Louie."

"I dun fotch your horse out in de pines dar," said the servant, waving his hand towards a thicket beyond the graveyard. "Miss Louie tole me to, sah."

" Why did she tell you to do so, Cæsar?"

"I dunno, sah; only she seemed powerful anxious that you should go away," he replied.

I read the card again. Poor Louie! I could do no less than grant this slight request. I tossed the servant a coin, and crossing the graveyard rapidly, entered the pines and found my horse. As I mounted, I heard voices in the direction I had come. I rode up to the edge of the pines to see what occasioned it. Standing on the very spot I had left but a few seconds before, were several of my cousins. It did not need the disconnected remarks which I caught, to tell me their object. Their knotted brows and angry gestures told enough. They had come to immolate the son at the mother's grave. The spirit was strong in me to rush back and defy them. But no, I would not engage in any broil at that time, especially with my kindred. The sight hardened me, however, beyond all power to be softened afterwards. I would fight them whenever they desired, after that day. They should find they could not trample upon me with impunity. Who were the De Jeunettes that they should thus presume to rule and dictate? Was not I one of them? Was not their imperious pride the badge and guarantee of my own free-dom of action? They should find that they had in me no unworthy enemy to contend with. So I rode away full of bitterer thoughts than I had known before.

Arriving at my office, I found fresh cause for excitement. Old Alec Bain, the uncle of Alice, was waiting there for me. After the ordinary salutations, he said:

"Well, Mr. Charles, I've come to say good-by. Just as I was afeard, that fresh has been the most unfort'nit one to us. The Mistis axed me to be sure and tell ye, though, that we didn't 'tach no manner of blame to you, Mr. Charles."

"What do you mean, Mr. Bain?" I asked, in astonishment.

"I knowed, Mr. Charles, that it wouldn't do no way for you to be thinking of our Allie, an' said so, you remember, at the time. Though I do believe that if two young critters ever loved each other, it's you and Allie. But it's too far atween, you see. You are too rich, an' she's too poor to have love grow and prosper, Mr. Charles."

"For Heaven's sake, Mr. Bain, explain your-self! I cannot understand you. Why are you

come to say, 'Good-by'?" I asked, going back
to his first enigma.

"Jes' cause I'm gwine," he replied.

"Going? Going where?"

"That's more'n I can tell ye. I'm gwine somewhere, if I kin, whar a white man, if he *is* poor,
can hold his own with his neighbors, let 'em be as
rich as they may. Allie's been writin' to us that
the North's a heap nigher bein' that sort of place
than we've ever hed any notion on. So I
'llowed we'd go up an' see her a bit and look
around. I doubt if we ever come back here
again. I'm satisfied, and always have been, for
that matter, that the South's no place for a poor
man. He's just got no place nor business here,
only jes' to be a sort of daubin' to fill the chinks
atween master and nigger."

"You do not mean that you are actually going
away, Mr. Bain?"

"Going away. If I live to see to-morrow night,
I'll take my first ride on a railroad train; that's
shore!"

"But what's the cause of this sudden move?"

"Don't you know, Mr. Charles?"

"Indeed I do not."

"Hain't you heard of anythin' that ought to

make old Alec Bain think of makin' himself scarce in this country?"

I assured him that I had not; and then he gave me a history of the past few weeks, which raised my anger to a pitch of fury before unknown. During that interval every horse and cow that belonged to the old man had been killed or maimed, and herds of cattle turned loose upon the corn bottoms which he had rented and was working himself.

"I knowed," he said, "almost from the first that it was the work of no one but your family, and told the Mistis so; I knowed they wasn't never going to forgive me for your chancin' to love my little Allie. I said, too, that there wasn't no sense in trying to make a fight with the De Jeunettes. I knowed they wasn't doing on't themselves, but just a crowd of low-down white trash, who will do their bidding, if they do 'risk the widder,' for the sake of a little money. An' even if I should manage to get them punished after a long time, I'd have nothing left myself for the stock I'd lost. So I concluded 'twas no use to mend what was broke, but just went to your father and told him what had happened, as if I hadn't any sort of idea who did it. He didn't

seem no way surprised; and when I said that I
had concluded to pick up and leave the plantation an' go off at once if we could agree on what
was fair in a settlement, he 'llowed I wasn't far
from right, and said he'd act liberally. Then he
asked me how much I thought he owed me, and
I put it pretty high, 'cause, as I said, I was toler-
able sure all this mischief hadn't been done to
me and he not knowin' nothin' of it, and then take
it so cool when I tole him on't. So, I said I
reckoned about six hundred dollars. He said my
crops and cattle both wasn't wuth that, but he
wouldn't make no words with me over it; but if
I'd go off and leave the State and take Allie
with me, and not come back, he'd give me eight
hundred. I agreed to the terms, and we start to-
morrow morning, airly."

"So," said I, "you have not only let these
tyrants run you out of the State, but have promised that Allie shall not return to it!"

" Not while she is under my control Mr. Charles.
Of course, I'm not responsible for her afterwards.
Though, if you and she both'll take my advice,
you'll keep as far from here as a fox from a
steel trap if he knows its whereabouts. They
may get over it with you, though I doubt it; but

there'll never be any peace for her here, no-how."

"Yes, there will, Mr. Bain," said I. "I will make it, and she shall come and enjoy it. They cannot drive me out. I'll fight them foot to foot, and hand to hand."

"But I hear you are cut off—disinherited," said he.

"Yes, that's true," said I, feeling for the first time what the fact portended: "Yes," said I bitterly, "I am almost as poor now as Allie was when I offered her my love. If she chooses to throw me off on that account, well and good. If it was Charles De Jeunette's money she accepted and not himself, I shall know it now."

"My Allie ain't one of that sort, Mr. Charles," said the old man proudly.

"No, I am sure she is not," I answered; "and as for the disinheritance, who cares for it? I am not one of the De Jeunettes who can do nothing for themselves. I have a good practice at the bar—enough for us to live on comfortably until I can make more."

"Yes," said the old man thoughtfully; "but you must remember that you gained that because you were a De Jeunette."

"True," said I defiantly, "and I will hold it because I am a De Jeunette, as strong at the bar as they in their broad acres and hundreds of slaves. They cannot put me down, as you will see."

"Well, I hope not, Mr. Charles; I 'spects your love for our Allie has brought trouble to you as well as to us. I told the Mistis so when I heard on't. We're mighty sorry for it, the Mistis and me, but we don't rightly see as we can be blamed, nohow. We hopes things'll come right somehow, and you'll be happy some time."

The old man wept as he held out his hand to say farewell.

"We shan't forget you, Mr. Charles, never, if we be a long way off an' 'mong strangers at that. The Mistis an' I'll always pray for ye every day, we will, Mr. Charles."

He wrung my hand and would have departed, but I held him back a moment and said:

"Mr. Bain, the year that I was to wait for Allie is not over; but I shall meet you at Maplewood when the term closes, and bring Allie back as my wife, unless she refuses me."

I think the old man had a lingering notion that I might give up his niece under all the pressure that was being brought to bear upon me, and was surprised at this declaration. At least he held my hand more tightly, and said :

"God bless you, Mr. Charles! God bless you! You *is* true if all the rest is false!" and was gone.

His parting words seemed like a benediction. I *would* be true. I had almost yielded to temptation, and was now beset with trial, but I would be true. Allie should never know that I had ever faltered. I was ashamed that I had. I would be true to her if it cost me a life-long fight—aye! if I lost the fight, and lost my life too!

CHAPTER VIII.

LOVER, OR FRIEND?

JUST off from the road that led from Childsboro'
to Belmont was the ruin of an old log church,
so old and forgotten that there was no memory or
record of its earlier existence among the inhab-
itants. Few, indeed, knew of it. It was on the
land of my uncle Charles, and, as I said, not more
than a hundred yards from the main road; yet I
well remember his look of surprise when, riding
by with him one day, I referred to its existence.
He could only be satisfied of the truth of my
statement by going himself to examine it. It
stood on the slope of a hill, where there was a
little plateau of level ground, and not far from
what had probably been a spring, though now a
small swamp whose densely grown outlet was between the church and the highway. Undoubtedly
this little miry branch, which ran in a sort of
semicircle forty or fifty yards from the church, had
been the means of securely hiding it for so long a
time. Back of it the hill rose sharply, and the

whole region in the rear was densely wooded for
a considerable distance. One side had fallen in,
but the solid logs of the other walls seemed to resist time's approaches with a conscious stubbornness. It had evidently been a large and well-
made structure for its day. The hearth and fire-
place were of huge pieces of soapstone, which must
have been drawn at least five miles, for there was
no quarry nearer. In front was a small open space
shaded by several giant oaks, which may have been
hitching-trees when the church was in use. On
one of the trees the end of a horseshoe was just
visible outside the bark, which had grown over it
since it was driven into the trunk. Back of the
house were a few graves—none knew whose, and
the headstones bore no record. The message
they brought to the living was an anonymous one.

This had been a favorite haunt with Louie and
myself when we were children. Many a day had
we played here in the shade—she listening to my
wild dreams, and interspersing her more subtle
thoughts with my vague aspirations. It was here
that she had appointed a meeting.

Her note had said ten o'clock, but it was little
more than nine when I pushed Sachem through
the thick growth of alders which skirted the miry

branch in front and galloped up the dark old
avenue which had once been the wagon road from
the church to the highway. I had purposely an-
ticipated the time, for the recent conduct of my
relatives had been such as to inspire me with suspicion of them all, even Louie. I tied Sachem in
a pine thicket, a hundred yards or more away, and
then went and sat down in the shadow of the old
ruin.

It was a glorious moonlight night, but I was
hardly in a mood to appreciate its beauty. Hardly
half an hour had passed when I heard the rattling
footsteps of a pony coming down the stony hill
and across the bottom from the direction of Belmont. It halted a moment before the old church
path, and then plunged into the bushes, splashed
across the branch, and came up the shaded avenue
and into the circle of light before the sinking
structure. It was Louie, upon her favorite pony,
and alone. Still I did not reveal myself. The
pony pricked up his ears, looked sharply in my
direction, snorted loudly once or twice, and then
probably recognizing my identity, dipped his head
and began grazing. Louie slipped from the saddle, looked at her watch by the moonlight, and
then flung herself at the foot of an old oak, bury-

ing her face in her hands. She was soon shaken
with sobs. I left my hiding-place, went to where
she was lying, and, bending over her, whispered,
"Cousin Louie!"

She sprang to her feet and threw her arms
about my neck.

"O Cousin Charles!" she cried, " why will you?
It is so horrible!" And her slight form was convulsed with shuddering sobs. I tried to soothe
her excitement, but in vain. She clung to me still
more closely, and exclaimed between her sobs:

"They will kill you, Cousin Charles! They
will kill you! Why do you act so? You know
how we all love you—how *I* love you—and now
—now, I can save you if you will only love me a
little! They would forgive your course to your
mother, though it was horrible, Cousin Charles;
but my brothers swear they will kill you for the
way you have treated me."

"Oh, I know," she continued impetuously, as I
tried to interrupt her. "You think yourself in
honor bound to marry that horrid overseer's girl,
but you must not, Cousin Charles! You do not
love her! You cannot love her—not as you do
Louie! O Charles! Charles! have I not been
yours, your little Louie, ever since I can remem-

ber? What can be strong enough to take you away from me? Am I not your wife to-night in all but name? Who but one who loved you more than all the world beside would have come here to warn you of your danger and save you from it? Oh! say that you will let that horrid creature go, and make me and all our people happy! Say you do not love her, that you will not marry her! Pray, pray do!"

She slid from my arms and knelt before me, clasping my knees. The moonlight poured upon her tear-stained face.

"Hush, hush, Louie," I cried; "you must not —you shall not speak thus to me!"

"But you will not marry that—that woman. You do not love her?" she cried pleadingly.

"I must, I do," I said firmly. "I am bound to her by every consideration of honor—by every pledge—short of marriage itself. You would not have me act dishonorably, Louie?"

"But have you not promised me a hundred times?"

"In childish sport, Louie. I hardly knew that you had grown to womanhood until I had pledged my word to Alice Bain."

"Do not speak her name!" she cried, springing

to her feet and thrusting her fingers in her ears. "I hate her! You would break faith with me, with your mother who is dead—who died of sorrow for your shame—for this overseer's brat!"

"Louie! Cousin Louie!"

"Bah! don't call me Cousin Louie—I hate you! You could lie to me year after year, but your word to this mean, low thing is sacred!"

"Cousin Louie!" I exclaimed, reaching forth to take her arms.

"Do not touch me!" she almost shrieked, as I caught her left arm. "Let me go!" she cried, struggling wildly. Then she raised her right hand and I heard her riding-whip hiss through the air, and felt the raw-hide cut into my cheek. She sprang upon her pony and dashed off. I sat down upon the broad stepping-stone and rested my head upon my hands. The blood trickled through my fingers. How long I sat there buried in distressing thoughts I do not know. I remember hearing the pony dash across the bridge, and Sachem whinnying after him. The next thing that attracted my attention was Louie dashing again into the circle of light that was around me, leaping from her pony and falling upon her knees before me as she cried:

"Forgive me, Cousin Charles! Forgive me! I did not mean it, but I do love you so that I was mad—yes, mad—wild with rage. Say you forgive me, Cousin Charles."

I threw my arms about her and kissed her, as I again and again assured her of a brotherly love, no less true than that other love I had given to her who was to be my wife.

Then as she sobbed upon my breast I told her the whole story of my love for Alice Bain, how it had grown and ripened, and how more than worthy she was of it. When she had heard all, she lay quiet in my arms awhile; then, raising her head, she put back her dark locks from her pale face, and said:

"You are right, Cousin Charles. I have been weak; but you have not done wrong. I cannot help loving you; but you are not to be blamed for not loving me—at least, not as much as I wish you could, for you must always love me a little, a very little, will you not?" she asked, as the tears flowed piteously. I soothed her as best I could, and then she continued: "But I came back to tell you that you must go away. Do not go to Childsboro' again. My brothers are there after you, and will surely kill you if you are found. I know you are brave, but so are they, and strong and active as well as you ; and they are four, while you are but one. Our cousins from Highmont and some others are there too ! Go away at once by some country road till you take the stage for the North. Promise me that you will do this!"

I gave the promise, and she went on :

"I am to be the heir of Beaumont, you know, Cousin Charles. I thought when I agreed to it at first that you would finally come to yield to the conditions. Since you cannot, remember that your children shall have it unimpaired whenever they shall ask it. I shall hold it always in trust for them."

With a last tearful embrace I placed the noble, impulsive girl upon her pony, and listened to the sound of his footsteps as he bore her homeward.

CHAPTER IX.

BROUGHT TO A FOCUS.

AS I had determined, I met Alec Bain and his wife at Maplewood, which was the name of the seminary that Allie was attending, somewhat before the time limited, and impetuously insisted on immediate marriage. She, poor timid dove, when she had heard as much as they were able and I saw fit to tell her of the difficulties at home, tearfully endeavored to persuade me to one of two courses: either to delay our marriage for another year, or to go North or West and begin in some young center of life and progress where men were esteemed for themselves and not for their ancestry. Of course I would not listen to her pleadings; her apprehensions only made me the more determined to beard the lion in his den, and conquer my family in the seats of their pride. Of course, too, she yielded. No, that is not the proper term, since it implies opposition, which she could not offer to my will or wishes. I mean that she gave up her entreaty, ceased endeavor-

ing to persuade me to use my reason, and prepared herself quietly and cheerfully to abide the
results of my headstrong folly.   So one pleasant
morning we were married there among strangers,
and bidding good-by to Alice's kind foster-parents,
we started out upon a long and happy wedding-
tour.   What I enjoyed as I watched her gratification during those halcyon months, it is needless
to say.   The happiest days must end, however,
and I had determined to be at home for court,
which came in the middle of October.   So we
watched the northern forest glow and fade, and
in the hazy Indian summer, when the leaves on
our native hills were ripening at leisure to the
hazel brown which the oak puts on before winter,
and the gums and poplars were flaming out the
gaudy defiance which they flaunt in the face of
death, we came to our home.   So we said as day
by day we drew nearer, each with an apprehension we would not breathe to the other.   At last
we reached Childsboro'.

We arrived on Saturday, and took lodgings at
the only hotel.   It rained on Sunday, and we
scarcely left our rooms.   The court sat on Monday week, so that I had but little time to prepare
my cases for the fall term.   I was accordingly

early at my office on Monday, awaiting my clients. The first man to enter my office that morning was Mr. Rolf, who had been my former partner.

"So you are back, Mr. De Jeunette," he said.

"Oh, yes," I answered gayly. "I have had my play, and have now come back to work."

"So I see," he rejoined moodily. He sat awhile, drumming on the table with a troubled look upon his face. Then he got up and closed the door, came and sat down in a chair before me, and said earnestly:

"Mr. De Jeunette, have I proved myself sufficiently your friend to speak freely to you?"

I hastened to assure him that I was not only willing, but anxious that he should do so.

"Then allow me to say, sir, that the best thing you can do is to close your office, come to my house, keep yourself out of sight until nightfall, and then leave the State!"

"And why, Mr. Rolf, should I take so extraordinary a course?"

"It is useless to beat about the bush in this matter. Your relatives are greatly exasperated over the unfortunate course you have adopted, and its still more unfortunate results," he said.

"I have only done what my conscience and manhood approved, and whatever may have been the result of my course, it is due not to its impropriety, but to the insatiate pride of my family."

"I did not speak of your acts as wrong, nor of their results as intended by you; but certainly the death of both your parents, following so closely upon a knowledge of your course, is sufficient to justify me in terming both, under the circumstances, unfortunate."

"My parents! You do not mean, Mr. Rolf, that my father is dead!"

"Yes," he answered. "He died soon after the news of your marriage reached us."

The people I had met had not spoken of this event, probably supposing me to be aware of it, while my family would have strictly refrained from all communication with me, even if any one of them had known my address since my marriage.

"You must see, Mr. De Jeunette, that this fact will add greatly to the hostility with which you were already regarded by your kin. Believe me, your life is in constant danger while you remain here."

"I am not a coward," I answered, "to be driven off by the threats of a few hot-blooded roys-

terers. I have done only what I had a right
to do, and have done it honorably, and I will
not be bullied on account of it by all the De
Jeunettes on earth. They know me, and they
will think twice before they attempt personal violence."

"They are as hot-headed as you are now prov-
ing yourself to be," said Mr. Rolf, "and as brave.
Now, what is the result if you stay here? You
know they will forget or forgive nothing you have
done, nor any evil which they may fancy to have
grown out of it. The consequence is that sooner
or later there must be a personal encounter.
You must kill or be killed—perhaps both. In
any event, you gain nothing but the satisfaction
—if such it be—of dying at the hands of your
own kindred or staining yours with their blood.
Should you die, you leave your young wife un-
provided for and at their mercy, and if you
survive you must either leave them or continue
on here with no advantage, but every disad-
vantage against you. I admit your right to
do as you intimate, but no one having any interest in your life or prospects could approve its
policy."

I had not looked at it exactly in that light, and

I could but admit that there was force in the view which he took of my situation.

Continuing, he said, "You are a young man without means, except your profession, and with the hostility of at least the most powerful connection in this entire section arrayed against you. Do you not see how much more the same effort would yield you elsewhere? This is quite ignoring the almost inevitable occurrence of one or more disgraceful family brawls, and the very great probability of a violent death. Now against this you can only put the gratification of having your own way. Besides, let me tell you what I believe is God's truth. To a young man without means or family to help him forward in the profession, the West or Northwest offers far greater advantages and a thousandfold more chances of success than can be found here."

Well, the result of our conversation was that I concluded to adopt his advice in part and reject the rest—the most important, as I well knew he regarded it. I would leave Childsboro', but not like a thief or a coward, driven away by my blustering cousins, but honestly and openly. After the court, when my business could be straightened up and settled, I would leave. Till then any De

Jeunette or any one else who wanted me might know where to find me.

The old man sighed when he heard my determination, but knew me too well to attempt to change it further.

"I only hope you may not regret having made it," he said solemnly, as he put on his hat and went out.

A few moments after the Sheriff of the county entered. His manner seemed somewhat constrained, I thought. After a short time he said, drawing a paper from his pocket,

"Mr. De Jeunette, I have a little matter here which must be attended to."

"What is that?" I asked.

"A *Ca. Sa.*," * he replied.

"Against whom?" I asked, thinking that some client had been *Ca. Sa*-ed during my absence, and required my aid.

"Against yourself."

"Against me?"

"Yes."

"For what amount?"

---

* *Capias ad satisfaciendum*: a writ requiring the defendant to be taken and held to bail for the payment of a debt.

" Something the rise of nine thousand dollars, principal money, and some interest, I don't know how much," he replied.

I saw at once my condition and realized its horror. The *Ca. Sa.* regarded not the condition or ability of the debtor. There were but three alternatives—the money, good security for the debt, or the body of the debtor. I did not have the first, and felt that I could not hope to obtain security for so large a sum. Indeed, when I came to look my situation squarely in the face, I was satisfied that I could not give security for a tithe of that sum. There was but one way left—the jail.

I wrote a brief note to Alice, telling her not to be alarmed at my absence, not to trouble herself about anything that might happen, and above all not to seek me until I should send her word explaining all that might seem surprising.

Then I took up my hat and said:

" Well, Mr. Sheriff, I will go with you."

" Do you not wish to give security?"

"You know I cannot."

" Would you not like to go by and see your wife?"

" No.   Give her that, please," handing him the note which I had just written.

So I locked my office-door, little thinking how or when I should enter it again, and went along the street with the Sheriff, until we found the sleepy jailer, who looked up at me with all the surprise of which his slothful nature was capable, as he took down the great key from a nail above the head of his bed and accompanied us to the jail. Poor man, it was some relief to him at any rate. It magnified his importance and gave him something to do; for the position of jailer was very nearly a sinecure in Childsboro'—thanks to the whipping-post, the stocks, and the branding-iron, which were the ordinary instruments of punishment and torture. At this time the institution was empty, and had been for some weeks, as he informed me during one of his frequent visits through the day.

Arrived at the jail, I was shown to the debtor's apartment, and the Sheriff, after begging my pardon for the performance of his duty, and directing his subordinate, in emphatic language, to attend to my wishes and provide for my comfort, withdrew.

The garrulous deputy filled the water-bucket, shook up the infested-looking bed, and inquired as to my wishes in regard to dinner. Seeing that I was inclined to take a somewhat melancholy view of the situation, he took up the *rôle* of comforter, and endeavored to beguile my loneliness with an account of some of my predecessors in those quarters.

"There was Mike Sherwood, now; he staid here nigh on to fifteen year. He learned shoe-making, or knew it afore he came, I disremember which, an' used to follow the trade here. That was afore my day, but I've heard my father tell on't often. He was jailer in his time many a year, perhaps all the time old Sherwood was in here. Ther was a Jedge staid here a smart bit, too. Yes, a Jedge!" answering my look of sur-prise, for I could not help taking a sort of interest in those tales of my forerunners in misery. "What! Never heard of it? Why, I 'sposed everybody knew that. Yes, a Jedge of the Superior Court of Law and Ekkity, ez the crier says when he calls it on. You've heard of *him* often enough, if not of his bein' here. Jedge Morphy, ye know, used to live up on the Ala-manee. He got in debt some way—I never knowed how—gamblin' or bettin', I suppose, for he had a mighty fine plantation, and might hev lived without doin' anything if he had only let

sech things alone. He was a mighty fine man.
I remember him well, and everybody pitied him,
when he got down, more'n any one I ever saw. I
do believe the people would hev paid his debts
for to get him out. I'm not sure but they did
jes' chip in and do it finally. The queerest thing
about it all was, that his biggest creditor became
his successor in office. But thar's quare things
in this world—quare things. Wal, I s'pose I'm
worryin' ye, so I'll take myself off. Don't be
downhearted. Ye'll either get out soon, or it'll
come to seem right home-like tu ye, bein' here.
Good-by."

He locked the huge door, and I was alone in
my dungeon, with a bitter past and a hopeless
future. He came again at noon and brought my
dinner and also a note from Alice, and a package.
The note ran thus:

"DEAREST:

"I have learned of your new trouble, but do
not understand its cause—only that you are imprisoned for debt; but I know it will all be right,
and that soon. I have been praying for you—
that you might not lose heart and hope, nor be
cast down by what seems so dreadful. Remem-

ber that while you are hopeful and brave your little Allie will not despair.   I do not see how I can
help you now except by praying for you ; but I
will try—oh ! so hard. · I send you my Bible—
the only dowry I brought you—and pray that its
quaintness, if not my love, may lead you to find
in its pages treasures which earth can neither give
nor take away.   After you, my beloved, this
dear old volume is the chiefest treasure of my
life.   I never think the Gospel is so sweet in any
other guise.   I learned to pick it out of the old
text when but a child.   Hoping it may comfort
you as it has often been blessed to me, I remain,
with countless prayers,

"Your devoted

"ALLIE."

The book which was thus sent was an old English Bible of one of the earliest editions ever
printed.   It was no doubt a very choice edition,
and regarded as a wonderful work of art in its
day.   And indeed some of its perfections have
never been excelled.   No printer of our modern
days could print those curious capitals and book-
headings in a red fairer or half so enduring, or
with a more perfect register.

It was bound, too, with the half-raw parchment which the binders of those old days knew so well how to manage, that closed over and protected the carefully-figured edges of the old volume. Poor child! I could but think, as I examined the ancient book, that the treasure she had probably picked up at some old bookstall must at some time have cost the possessor a fortune, though there seemed no chance of its present owner finding one in it.

This volume was enclosed in a soft case of purple velvet, old and much worn in places, but retaining its richness and depth of color in others. It had been embroidered by deft hands, and in the middle of one side, in letters like those within, was the name "Nellie," faded, yet distinct ; while in one corner, in a compartment, as it were, of the embroidery, in clear letters and undimmed colors, evidently wrought by her own hand, was the name "Allie."

I had made these discoveries and looked through the volume, reading here and there a passage which seemed wonderfully fresh and captivating in its quaint habit, when, turning back to the beginning of the book, my eye rested on the name *John Eax.*

It was the signature of an inscription on the first blank page in the book,

> "*To my beloved daughter Nell,*
>
> "JOHN EAX,"

and written under it was the name of one of those English cities where busy hammers have forged miracles of progress, and built up a metropolis **that queens it in the world of mechanic art as easily as Athens once ruled in the domain of the beautiful.**

CHAPTER X.

A TROUBLED NIGHT.

AS the sun went down and darkness came upon me, I forgot for a time, in the terrible depression of solitary confinement, the puzzle of the daylight over this haunting name, with which my story opened. The misfortunes which my situation indicated pressed upon my mind, and I ran over a thousand times the possibilities of the past and the future.

I was in custody upon various writs of *Ca. Sa.*, issued at the instance of Bill Letlow, a noted bill-shaver of the region, who held the notes upon which I was security for Fred Wiley, as well as some that I had given myself. I had always thought Fred would pay those which I had incurred in his behalf, or, if not, that his father would. At all events, I had received so many favors from his father that I could not refuse the son, and with Beaumont and the De Jeunette family and fortune behind me, the amount was a mere bagatelle. I was satisfied that a large part of this indebtedness was incurred at the gaming-table, but was unable to prove the fact, as Fred had gone to parts unknown some time before my arrest. His father, I knew, was entirely unable, because of recent losses, to discharge these debts, and Bill Letlow had the reputation of never loosening his grip while a shred of property or pound of flesh was in his reach.

Under these circumstances I could see but one way out of my present confinement, and that was by the Insolvent Debtor's oath—a proceeding which involved at least a month's imprisonment, and might perhaps, by a captious creditor, be made to require a year. Besides, it was attended by an amount of disgrace that can scarcely be realized in our later days of wide-spread bankruptcy and financial dishonor. I could only look forward to a ruined life—a life of penury and dishonor for my wife and our children. How bitterly did I regret my obstinate refusal to listen to my young wife's entreaties not to return to Childsboro'.

It was about nine o'clock when I was interrupted in these melancholy musings by the entrance of Dick Birney, the Sheriff, and his jailer. They looked around the room with some care, and seemed anxious, as I thought, about something of importance. At length the Sheriff spoke :

."Have you any arms about you, Mr. De Jeunette?" he asked.

So they had come to search me and prevent my escape. Indeed I had fallen very low for a De Jeunette.

"I beg pardon," I said, seemingly indifferent. "I am so little used to this sort of thing that I was not aware that it was necessary for a gentleman to surrender his pocket-knife and toothpick when imprisoned for debt. I am very sorry to have put you to this trouble, though I could have assured you that it was unnecessary. I had no intention of breaking out."

"Pshaw!" said Dick. "You have known me long enough, Charley De Jeunette, not to take me for a fool. I did not come here to disarm you, but to inquire if you are armed."

Owing to the threats of my cousins, I had prepared myself for an encounter before leaving the hotel that morning, and still had my arms about me. So I answered in some surprise :

"I am—fully," and taking a revolver from my pocket I laid it upon the table by him.

"All right, all right," said he, pushing it to-

wards me. "Keep it, you are more likely to
need it than I. And by the way, Tom and I have
concluded to stay down here to-night and keep
you company. Not wishing to trouble you, we
shall sleep in the passage."

"Dick Birney," said I, "you surely do not
expect me to escape, that you are taking all this
precaution."

"I do not fear an escape, but a rescue," he
replied seriously. "You know your family have
a bad name for helping each other out of
limbo."

"You need not be afraid of my family taking any such trouble on my account," said I,
smiling.

"Not as a favor, I am aware, Mr. Charles; but
love is not the only passion that sometimes un-
locks prison-doors."

"My God! Mr. Birney. You don't mean—"

"You ought to know why your family would
be particularly anxious to get you out of this
place," he interrupted.

"And you—"

"I am going to resist. No man or set of men
shall ever take a prisoner from my hand for love
or hate except in due form of law. I said that

long ago, and have stuck to it pretty well thus far. Presuming that you wouldn't object to helping a little on such an occasion, I intended offering you arms if you had none. I do not expect, however, to need your aid, nor even to be compelled to fight; but you De Jeunettes are mighty determined men, and I may have trouble. You will have no need of weapons, however, until after Dick Birney's dead. If it comes to that, you may be in tight quarters."

Birney and the jailer withdrew, and I tried to realize the full horror of my situation. To add to my other ills, my relatives were desirous of taking me from the hands of the law, that they might lynch me.

Towards midnight I heard the tramping of many feet before the jail. A moment after and a huge stick of timber was borne against the door, which gave way before it like a reed.

Then I heard Dick Birney's voice ring out clear and strong:

"Gentlemen, I expected this visit, and am prepared for it. Not one of you can enter that door alive without my permission. Now, what are your wishes?"

There was a moment of silence, and then something was said from without. I did not catch the words, but the Sheriff answered :

"He is in the custody of the law, and no man shall take him out, unless he passes over my dead body, or pays the debt for which he was arrested."

"How much is the debt?" asked a voice, presently.

"About ten thousand, interest and cost," was the reply.

"Who holds the papers?"

"Bill Letlow."

"How long will you keep him if the debt is not paid, Sheriff?"

"Till he rots, unless he takes the insolvent's oath."

"Ah, bah!" burst in a voice I recognized at once as that of one of my cousins, "he'll never do that. He's a De Jeunette if he *is* a scoundrel, and as proud as Lucifer. He'll never swear out!"

"Dunno," said the Sheriff. "I'd sooner bet on that than on Bill Letlow loosing his hold."

"You're right there, Sheriff. The jail would tumble in before that could happen."

There was a sort of half-silence for a little time.

Those outside were evidently consulting. Then
the voice that was unknown to me, probably some
tool of my cousins', called out again :

"You say, Sheriff, that if the debts were paid
off you'd let him go?"

"Of course I would. No right to hold him a
minute after that."

"Would an order from Bill Letlow do?"

"Yes, if the costs were paid too. I ain't going
to risk Letlow for them."

"Well, we're going to have the man, but we
don't want to trouble you, if we can help it, Mr.
Sheriff. Besides, the rascal's debts ought to be
paid for the sake of his name. Good-night!"

"Well, they're mighty cool about it!" said the
Sheriff, putting up his weapons, as they moved
away.

Then I heard them shutting and temporarily
fastening the door, which had been beaten open,
and soon after their loud breathing showed me
that they were sound asleep. For me, I could
not sleep. My brain was on fire with wild and
desperate thoughts. I could see no light, no
hope. The future was as dark as the night that
was around me. I paced back and forth in my
cell in restless agony. Then I sat down by the

table and rested my head on my folded arms.
As I did so my hand touched the old Bible still
lying on the table in its velvet case, and the name
of John Eax rose in my mind. My weary and
confused brain seemed to seize upon it at once as
a means of relief from its terrible strain. Gradually, from thinking of the possibilities of the
future to Alice and myself, I began to run off
into conjectures upon the personality of this
myth who had crossed my perturbed consciousness with such a persistent idea of old acquaint-
anceship attached to him. So little by little I
forgot my woes, and became absorbed again in en-
deavoring to answer the seemingly vain question:
" Who is—or was—John Eax?" From this
speculation I passed unconsciously into slumber,
and dreamed of John Eax and Alice and myself
in strangely connected relations. The bluff old
Englishman seemed to have my little Alice under
special care and to be offering an effectual relief
to my difficulties. I could never remember the
particulars of that strange dream, but it left so
vivid an impression on my mind that when I
awoke it was with that feeling of relief which
confident hope brings to despair, and I lay down
and slept soundly until morning.

CHAPTER XI.

IT was with surprise that I found myself, on awakening the next morning, able to eat the breakfast that was brought me by the jailer, and to regard the future with so little of gloomy apprehension. I sent to Alice a note which was really hopeful, telling her to be trustful and quiet; that all would be right eventually; that her memento had been more comfort to me than she could have expected; which, indeed, was literally true, but not in the sense that I knew she would understand it. Yet I felt no compunctions in regard to the little fraud I was perpetrating on her credulity. I knew she would consider this and the whole tone of my letter as an evidence that I had found a religious consolation in its pages. She had engrafted upon her tender, clinging nature all the stern, harsh creed of her Scottish ancestry, accompanied by their clear and vivid idea of the personal indwelling of the religious principle—a sort of sixth sense—only to be

acquired by a kind of complex miracle. Our faith
—that of the De Jeunettes—had approximated
more nearly to a matter-of-course acceptance of
the doctrines of Christianity, without any especial
consideration of its application or personal character. I had never thought of religion as a
serious business; and I knew my little Allie,
with her simple faith, had made my religious
apathy a subject of frequent prayer, almost from
the first moment of our acquaintance. I knew
she would take my language as indicating an
answer to her petitions, and that her sweet soul
would burst out into a quiet, tearful song of
adoration and gratitude for it. I could but
smile sorrowfully as I prepared this kindly decep-
tion; and yet the dear child's book had given me
a distraction which relieved my strained mind
from a tension that must ere long have led to
insanity; I had not been in the 'mood to find its
deeper treasures.

Still my mind was full of John Eax, and I was
determined if possible to ferret out the particular
manner in which I had become familiar with his
name. I had always been noted for methodical
habits in my studies and business, and I therefore
thought it probable that if I had ever known any-

thing worth remembering about this puzzling
individuality, memory, dream, or whatever it
might be, that I would be able to find a note of
it among some of my memoranda. I therefore
requested the Sheriff to bring from my office my
commonplace-book of correspondence. In this,
it had been my custom to enter a minute of the
writer's name, date, and substance of every letter
which I received. I sent also for some miscel-
laneous commonplace-books in which I had been
accustomed to enter matters which were of interest rather than value in my professional studies
and practice. All of these books were carefully
indexed.

Immediately upon their arrival I sat down to in-
spect the indexes. One after another I ran over
them in vain. The name of *John Eax* had certainly not been signed to any letter which I had
received, nor did it occupy a prominent place in
any of the memoranda of the commonplace-books.
It was probable, then, if I was not utterly mistaken, that it would appear as an item in some of
the abstracts of the letters I had received. I set
myself, therefore, to reading these entries, from
the last backwards. Page after page I read, turning them hopefully at first, I knew not why, and

then slower and slower, reading each entry in their crowded columns carefully.

It was well toward night, when I had quite despaired, that I found this entry:

"PLUMMER & OSGOOD, Solicitors,
　　　　Temple Street, London,
Want heirs of John Eax, supposed to be in America, if there are any."

It was in a commonplace-book that I had kept when first commencing the study of law, and was probably made from some advertisement which had met my eye. It had been indexed under the attorney's name, whence the difficulty I had in finding it. I had evidently made the entry with the vague, boyish anticipation that I might some time have need for the address in regard to the matter. It must have been a very indefinite idea, for even now that I had found the entry in my own hand, I could recollect nothing in regard to my object or motive in making it, nor why I had been led to take any notice of it at all.

While I sat thinking over this matter, I was somewhat surprised by the entrance of the Sheriff. I noticed, on his sitting down opposite me at the table, that he seemed not a little excited for one of his somewhat stolid temperament.

"Mr. De Jeunette," he said, "you believe that I am your friend?"

"I never had a doubt of that, Dick. You must not feel that I harbor any malice against you for doing your duty," I replied.

"Oh! I don't mean that. Of course, I do my duty, or try to, which is nearly the same; but do you trust me as a friend?"

"Certainly I do."

"Would you do whatever I might advise you to do for your own interest, without asking any questions?"

I looked him keenly in the eye, and answered, "I think I would, Dick."

"Very well, then. You will break out of jail to-night."

"Break out of jail? I do not understand you!"

"So much the better. You have agreed to follow my advice without question. Take hold here."

He took one end of the light bedstead and I the other, and lifted it out from the wall.

"There," continued Dick, pointing to a place where the mortar seemed newer than any other;

"that's the breaking-out place. There have been quite a number of escapes from this room, though nary one before this in my time. In fact, I don't believe there has been one in twenty years that somebody didn't know it afore it was done. That's where Sherwood is said to have got out. *I* think he went through the door; but it's a convenient thing for any one else. It has never been more than half built up. The mortar is more like the daubing of a log-house than a cement intended for strength.

"Now," he continued, drawing from beneath his coat a couple of large files, "here are the tools. They happen to be the best I could chance on at the minute, and one way and another will answer very well. Take out all but the outer course of brick at once, and pile them carefully under your bed to look as if you had been preparing this thing. Don't let the jailer have any suspicions when he comes with your supper. Keep at your book there, and be as down-hearted as you please. At eight o'clock kick out the last course, crawl out, and go down the run back of the jail till you come opposite the church-lot; there turn off to the right, and in the grove back of Lanier's you will find your blood-bay, Sachem, ready for a canter. You will find something you need in your saddle-bags. Don't let the grass grow under his feet until you get on the train for the North."

"But, Alice?" I asked anxiously. "What of her?"

"Alice knows all about it, and is on her way to Wilmington, where she will sail for New York. You see I ought to hold a grudge against you for marrying her, for I had been casting sheep's eyes at her a year before you ever saw her. I don't, though; and I could not see her take on without helping you, if I could do it safely, which I think I can. Besides that, those kin of yours are as murderous and revengeful as Comanches, and are bound to have your blood. Now, I've no notion of having you killed on my hands just for having married Alice Bain, though if I thought she would ever be a Bathsheba, I might be tempted to make you my Uriah, eh? But there's no chance of that, so she has gone to Wilmington to-day to throw your cousins off the track. It may not do, however; so you must not trifle on your way. You had better be lively."

"But you—how will this affect your interest?" I asked.

"Oh, hang my interest!" said he; "besides,

you promised not to ask any questions. But I must go now. Remember and keep this from Tom, when he comes. I may want him to do some swearing for me."

"God bless you, Dick," said I, as I gave him my hand. "God bless you for what you are doing. Good-by!"

"Good-by!" said he, with husky cheerfulness, "and better luck and kinder neighbors where you settle next."

He shut the door and was gone.

I worked steadily until I had removed the two inner courses of brick and hid the débris, then waited for the jailer, my supper, and eight o'clock —all of which came in due time. While I waited, I had copied the memorandum in the common-place-book, and wrapped Allie's Bible in a piece of coarse brown paper, being determined to take it with me.

As the clock in the Court House steeple began striking eight, I removed carefully the outer course of brick. By the time it ceased striking, the opening was clear, and after looking out, I jumped down, with my revolver in one hand and Allie's Bible in the other—for I am ashamed to say that I had half suspected that Dick Birney had spoken more truth in his jest about Uriah and his wife than in all the rest of the conversation. I was not molested, however, and found my way as speedily as possible to the grove, where I found Sachem, as I had been told. Then my suspicions vanished. I mounted him, and before morning was in R——. I left the horse at a stable in the city, and took the five o'clock train for the North. The railroad itself was a slow coach in those days, but in due time I reached New York and met Alice.

CHAPTER XII.

SOLUTION.

I FOUND five hundred dollars in the saddlebags on Sachem, with a note in Dick's handwriting saying it was in payment for the horse, which he had long wanted.

Alice was greatly pleased at my having brought back her Bible. But for her joy in seeing me I think she would have been still more demonstrative over the old volume.

" And was it truly a comfort to you, Charles, in that terrible prison ?" she asked anxiously.

" Yes, dear," I answered seriously. " A very great comfort indeed. But where did you get it ?"

" Where did I get it ? Why, it was my mother's and her mother's before she was married. Here is our family record—so far as we know it, that is —on my mother's side. Did you not see it ?"

" I had not noticed it," I said.

" You see," she said, " my mother always told me that her mother was the daughter of a rich man in some English manufacturing town, who had two daughters, my grandmother and one whose name I never knew. Her name was Ellen —Ellen Eax. She married Robert Jennings, who was a poor man, some sort of an artist I should judge from what has been told me. At least it was in opposition to the wishes of her father, who refused to assent to their marriage, and drove her from his house afterwards. They came to this country when it was new, just before the war of the Revolution, I believe, and soon afterwards both died. My mother was an infant at that time, and was left in the care of a neighbor, whose son she married when she grew up. She died long ago, leaving me, her youngest and only surviving child."

I gathered from her all that she knew of her parentage, the places where her mother and grandmother had lived, and then wrote to Plummer & Osgood to inquire why they wanted to hear of the heirs of John Eax. I learned in reply that John Eax had died in 1783, and had left a handsome estate which the heirs of Ellen Eax, his daughter, if any were living, were entitled to receive.

Well, the result of it was, that with some little difficulty I completed the chain of proofs which showed my little Alice, the overseer's niece, to be the great-granddaughter of John Eax, the Birmingham manufacturer who had left an immense fortune for the daughter whom he had driven out. I did not let Alice know of it until it was all over, and the decree in her favor signed. Then I procured a copy and put it between the leaves of her Bible. When she found it I told her it was her dowry that she sent me in the prison.

The fortune of John Eax was, however, coupled with one condition, namely: that the husband of his daughter, or her sons, or the husband of any female heir who might be entitled to take under his will, should, in such event, assume the name of *Eax*. With which condition it was by no means difficult for me to comply.

The difficulties which I had experienced from a lack of money since leaving Childsboro', connected with a remembrance of the fact that my relatives had twice attempted my life and were now dwelling in luxury while I was almost in penury, did not tend to foster a very warm attachment to the name of De Jeunette. In fact, my feelings towards my relatives were so bitter that I felt a malicious pleasure in throwing off the last mark

of relationship with them. It was a sort of retali-
ation for my dishonor and expulsion from the
clan. As soon as the necessary formalities could
be effected, therefore, I ceased to be a De Jeunette
and became John Eax; for it was my notion, instead of taking merely the name of Eax, to assume
the entire name of the man who had proved our
benefactor.

For a few years we traveled a great deal abroad,
yet we hesitated to settle down upon the Continent, and neither of us was inclined to remain
in the land from whence our good fortune was
derived. The fact is, we were both of us
thoroughly American, and had no wish to be
otherwise. Besides, I think Alice saw that my
old thirst for dominance and leadership among
men had not all died out, and desired that it
should be gratified. So we came back to America
and invested what was left of Alice's dowry in one
of the fresh, new States of the North-west, some
of it well, and some ill. As years went on, however, and the fetters of home were wrought about
us, it increased until I became master of an estate
which would have made that of which I had been
deprived seem dwarfish and mean. I had grown
with the young State, too, and honors and power

had come in no small measure to the fortuitous namesake of John Eax.

In the midst of my prosperity, however, Alice was stricken with disease and taken from me, leaving only her memory, full of blessed light, and a childish reflex of her own beauty in our young daughter, Alice Louise, to cheer my solitude. Before she died she called me to her bedside, and said:

"You have often wondered, no doubt, at the obstinacy with which I contended that our child should be called Louise. This letter will explain it to you. Read it when I am gone."

It was an old letter from Cousin Louie, dated on the day of my arrest in Childsboro', and was as follows:

"MY DEAR MADAME: Do not be distressed at the arrest of your husband. Learning that certain parties were determined to take his life, if not prevented, I put his notes, which I had previously had bought up for me at a great discount, into the hands of a noted money-lender named Letlow, who is simply acting as my agent in this manner, and as your husband's friend. While he is in jail he is safe from a greater evil, and we will

find some way to get him off. You can trust
Sheriff Birney, who is a true friend of your
husband. Permit me to request that you will not
inform Cousin Charles of my connection with the
matter.

"I am, faithfully,

"LOUISE DE JEUNETTE."

This letter explained what had hitherto been
somewhat mysterious to me, both in the events
which had then occurred, and in Alice's stout
championship of my cousin Louie.

Soon after this, came on the war. The North-
west had made me one of her most devoted sons.
The free, untrammeled life, the fierce, wild rush
of business, its intense earnestness and devotion
to progress and principle, fascinated me. I had
little reason for gratitude or tenderness towards
that portion of the nation which considered itself
aggrieved, though it was the place of my nativity.
For its peculiar principles and institutions I had
never much regard. Even when proud of being
a De Jeunette I did not believe slavery to be
right; and now that the free chill wind of lake
and prairie had cleared my brain of the mist of
interest and habit, I knew it was wrong, fearfully

wrong, wrong in the abstract, and still more
wrong in the concrete, wherever it touched any
class or nation, a wrong to the soil of the South,
to the slave, to the master, to the poor white. I
did not wish to fight against my relatives, but I
had ocular demonstration that they would not
hesitate to take my life, even without the excuse
of public war. So I put aside this scruple, and
was one of the first who offered themselves to
put down rebellion.

I was given command of a regiment, and before
the close of the war had attained a generalship.
When the surrender came, my division was
encamped in the vicinity of my native place, and
my own quarters were in Childsboro'. It was an
odd feeling that I had during those few weeks
of unlimited power among the seats of the De
Jeunettes. How often I smiled as I signed my
orders, " John Eax, Brevet Major-General Com-
manding Second Division," at the thought of the
invisible name it hid and the individuality that
was lost in it. But this was all the revenge I
took. I did think strongly once or twice of
having my cousins brought before me and dis-
covering myself to them—a sort of Joseph in the
Egypt which had come to them. When I made

inquiry, however, I found that several of them had died as brave men should die, and that others were even yet suffering from wounds received in the struggle. Of course, I gave up the idea at once, and was really ashamed that I had ever cherished one so silly. But then some foolishness may be pardoned to one who experiences such contrasts as that between my departure from Childsboro' and my return to it.

I satisfied myself experimentally with Dick Birney, the Sheriff. It was fifteen years since my departure; and a life of action, with some suffering, as well as the wounds, campaigning, and exposure of the war, had aged me and changed me no little, though I had hardly expected that my identity would remain undiscovered—perhaps had hardly desired that it should. Under pretense of making some inquiries in regard to the county, I sent for Dick Birney and asked many questions about the different families on plantations near the town. Among others, I asked about Beaumont.

"That place," said Birney, "is owned by Miss Louie De Jeunette, willed to her by old Peter De Jeunette."

"Her father, I suppose?" I said.

" No, her uncle. It was a curious thing, but she got one of the finest estates in the county by it." And then he went on and gave me a full narrative of myself from his standpoint. When he had concluded, I asked in an indifferent tone:

" How does it happen she has never married?"

" Now you are asking me a question which has grown old in Erie County, and never found an answer yet. Some say it is because she is too proud, and thinks herself too good for any sort of a man, and others that she was dead in love with her cousin Charles and cannot get over the disappointment of his marrying another. I don't consider that of any account, for she was not more than sixteen or eighteen when he went away. Besides, she looks and acts like anything but a disappointed woman. It seems to me that she grows fresher and fairer every year.

" What do the family say of her course?" I asked.

" None of them presume to criticise Queen Louie, I assure you," he replied. " She certainly rules the family as easily as if she wore a crown and they were her subjects."

As I had received all the information I cared about, I closed the conversation without his hav-

ing a suspicion of the real identity of the man
with whom he had been talking.

I determined to see my cousin Louie, and was
seized with an irrepressible desire to know whether
she would penetrate the mask which time and circumstance had placed upon me.

So a few days afterward I rode to Beaumont,
and sent in my card, requesting a brief interview
upon business of importance.

I was ushered into the old parlor, which seemed
unchanged since my earliest remembrance, and
in a few moments Cousin Louie entered. Good
reason had Dick Birney to say that time had not
robbed her of any charm, while it had brought
many more. She had that evident scorn for all
who wore the blue that all the ladies of the South
took such delight in showing at that day. Her
greeting was cold and distant, as she inquired to
what she was indebted for the unexpected honor
of my presence.

"Your name is Miss Louise De Jeunette," I
inquired doubtfully, consulting a memorandum,
as if to ascertain a fact not within my own knowledge.

"It is, sir."

"Pardon me, madam; but will you allow me

to ask if this letter was written by you?" said I, handing her the letter which she had written to Alice.

No sooner had she recognized it than her face showed the utmost excitement.

"How did this come into your possession?" she inquired.

"It was given me by the person to whom it was addressed, on her dying bed," I answered.

"You knew her, then?"

"Intimately."

"And did you know her husband—"

"Her husband? I was her husband."

"You—her husband?" she cried, starting up and coming towards me. "Then—"

She tottered and would have fallen, but I sprang forward and caught her in my arms.

"Cousin Louie," I cried, "do you not know me?"

"O Cousin Charles, I—I thought—you were dead," she exclaimed, as the tears ran over her eyelids. "Why did you try to make me think you were that odious Yankee, General Eax?"

"I have the honor to be no less a personage," I replied.

"Oh, you cannot deceive me any more. I know

you now. You are my cousin Charles De Jeunette, whom I am very glad to see—despite his
disguise," she said, resuming at once the demeanor of hostess, and motioning me to a seat
beside her on the sofa.

"I *was* Charles De Jeunette, I *am* John Eax!"

"In disguise," she interrupted archly.

"In very truth," I replied.

"I do not understand you. How can your
words be true?" she asked.

Then I told her the whole story of my life since
she had known it.

"But how could you fight against the South?
How could you join the Yankees?" she asked, as
I concluded.

"You forget, Cousin Louie," I replied, "that I,
of all men, had little reason to think kindly of the
South. Excepting you, there was hardly one in
its borders to whom I owed either gratitude or
affection, let alone the principles which were involved and the national life which was imper-
iled."

"You do not mean to say that you have become a Yankee in fact, and believe that you all
were in the right to oppress and rob the poor
South?"

"I am all that my uniform imports," I answered quietly—"no more, no less!"

"Then you have indeed ceased to be a De Jeunette," she said hotly, "and I thank God for it!"

"As I have done many thousand times," was my response.

"I think you might at least have retained enough of the gentleman not to come here and insult me, sir," she cried.

"Gently, Miss Louie," I replied. "I came here, in the open day, wearing the uniform which showed my rank and proclivities, to thank you for your kindness to me at another time, which was unknown to me until that letter was placed in my hands, and to ask the amount of my indebtedness to you. I had no intention or desire to argue with you the past or present, and, as you well know, am quite incapable of insulting you. As to being a renegade De Jeunette, the taunt has lost its force. Allow me to ask in what amount I am your debtor?"

"None at all," she answered half sullenly.

"You will not tell me?"

"I tell you, you owe me nothing, sir!"

"That makes it my duty to pay you, dollar for

dollar, with interest, the amount of the obligations you paid off for me."

" I will not touch your money."

" As you choose."

" Do you think after receiving Beaumont and all the property which should have been yours, and enjoying its use and profits so many years, I would touch the money which you acquired by renouncing your family and country!" she exclaimed, with tears springing to her eyes.

" That family had already disowned me."

"You know I always thought that was wrong, and have ever felt like an intruder in this house."

" My parents had a right to dispose of their property as they chose ; and having given it to you, it is yours without condition or limitation. But I must pay my own debts. Here is the amount of all the claims on which I was sued by Bill Letlow, at your instance, with interest to this date." I laid a pile of bills before her as I spoke, and added : "You will please count them and give me a receipt."

"I will not touch it. You shall not force your money upon me in that way ;" and she pushed it from her.

" What !" I said, as if in surprise. "You will

not give me a receipt when I offer you the money for my just debt? Perhaps you want specie."

"I don't want anything!—you know I don't!" she cried in a rage.

"But I cannot be trifled with in this manner, madame. A debtor has rights, and I must assert mine. If you will not give me a receipt, I must call in one of my staff, to witness the payment— or tender."

I stepped to the door and said, "Orderly!"

"Sir," replied the soldier, who was sitting on the porch.

"Ask Captain Westcott to step here for a moment."

The soldier saluted, and went down the steps towards the end of the avenue, where two or three of my staff were in waiting.

Louie saw him, and turning towards me, with tears in her eyes, and her hands clasped, said:

"Please, Cousin Charles—please don't! Take back your money, and don't make a foolish scene here. Please do!"

She came close to me and looked up beseechingly, her great brown eyes full of tears.

"Upon one condition only, Cousin Louie."

"What is that?" she asked, with a sigh of relief.

"I would rather do anything than have this foolish quarrel made public. I cannot take your money. You know that. Take it away!"

"It is, that I shall take my Cousin Louie with it."

"O Cousin Charles!" she exclaimed; but her face lighted up with a flaming blush, and her eyes gathered a softer light. "You know I cannot."

"The Captain's coming," I said.

"Oh, I—you are too bad," she said, wringing her hands and letting her head fall upon my breast, "to take advantage of me so."

"Do you consent?" I asked.

"Yes."

The Captain's steps were heard approaching the porch. I gave her one kiss, swept the money into my pocket, and went out to meet him. I managed to detain him a moment, that she might remove the traces of agitation, and then went with him into the parlor. She had taken a spray of her favorite honeysuckle from the mantel, and was pulling it in pieces—her face radiant with happiness.

"Captain," I said, "allow me to present to you Miss Louie De Jeunette, my affianced wife."

Louie was covered with a pretty confusion, but

the Captain's consternation was overwhelming. There was nothing to do but to bow and endeavor to hide it, which he did.

Making some excuse for having brought him in, I gave him some orders for the day, and directed him to return to camp, as I should stay to dinner, and sent him back to retail the marvelous news to his fellows, and, in short, to the entire command.

There was no delay in consummating the engagement thus suddenly initiated. Our cousins were in high dudgeon at Louie's course in marrying a "Yankee," and we did not deem it necessary to add to their hostility by revealing the metamorphosis which had taken place. In revisiting with Louie the scenes which had been familiar to our childhood, I learned the value of a bed of ore which lay on our land; and partly to please Louie, and partly with a hope of seeing the solitudes peopled and prosperous like the busy haunts of the North, we came back again to Beaumont. The whole story gradually leaked out, and was a nine days' wonder, and then passed away into the commonplace past. My relatives were first angry at my change of name, then regretful, and finally resigned.

There is but one thing more. My children illustrate one of the strange revenges which Time effects, and by which the future makes recompense so often to the past. My golden-haired Louie, Alice's child, the lineal descendant of the English shovel-maker, is likely to become the mistress of Graymont, and, with God's blessing, become the mother of De Jeunettes; while the third John Eax, a sturdy three-year-old, leans on "Cousin Louie's" lap and calls her "mamma."

————

The night had fallen as we sat and smoked upon the porch of the grand old mansion while Charles De Jeunette told the strange story of his inherit-ance. The ceaseless rumble of the unwearied water-wheel came up from the river bank a mile away, while the glare of the furnace fire upon the opposite hill-side lighted up the cedars of Beaumont. The namesake of the Birmingham manufacturer, filled with the spirit of the great North-west, was at once exacting tribute from the land of his birth, and repaying her a thousandfold for what he took. The kindred home-sites had fallen away in mag-nificence, and the neighboring plantations showed

the lack of prosperity.   The hedge-rows were up-
grown and the ditches clogged.   The old South
was dying around us.   The new South was springing into life about us—the spirit of the North
and the manhood of the South its matchless
elements.

THE END.

Mamelon.

MAMELON.

CHAPTER I.

BIRDS OF PARADISE.

IT was St. Valentine's Day, and a group of
merry girls with fair hair, light eyes, and
restless, eager ways, unwilling refugees from the
storms and routs of a Northern winter, were gathered in reckless abandon on the sunny back veranda of a Florida hotel. Camp-chairs, rockers, a
lounge or two, and numberless ottomans afforded
us resting places as we chatted and laughed and
basked in the soft, delicious sunshine of the semi-
tropic spring. The balmy breeze which had come
over forest and savanna far enough to have lost
the briny sharpness with which it left the coral
keys, had gathered a hint of the hot, mephitic
odors of the early blossoming vines of the everglades, and greeted us with a dreamy languor.

There was a kind of sentiment, an undertone,

as it were, of invalidism among us. Almost our sole brunette, the queenly and peerless Effie, who reclined upon the green rep lounge as on a throne, the most rollicking and reckless spirit among us, with great liquid eyes full of audacious mirth, had yet the skin of silky softness and the bloomy cheek which we all knew to be precursors of the fatal hectic. The most of us, however, were simply tired. The rush and cram, the unremitting excitement and restless ambition of American school-girl life, were just over. Nearly all of us had graduated the summer before. No wonder we were tired. Nature was revenging itself upon our overwrought young frames. So we were sent down into this delightful desert by anxious fathers, careful mothers, and sometimes, as we maliciously whispered amongst ourselves, through the machinations of those who were little inclined to a barefoot reel at the nuptials of a younger sister. So while we waited and recuperated we dreamed lazily of coming conquest.

Of the elder ladies who were with us younglings in this social Patmos our bevy was usually hardly respectful. They were dowagers and female Cerberuses—so we called them—mammas and aunts, or wives with sick husbands, literary old maids, or widows who had exhausted the ordinary arts of conquest, and betaken themselves to the desperate chances which a fashionable sanitarium might afford. All of them were tabooed by our merry clique, whose undisputed kingdom in fair weather was this second story back veranda—all except one.

She was a small, lithe woman, of a rich warm complexion, a wealth of soft brown hair, arched eyebrows, dimpled chin, and cheeks whose tender glow seemed to bid defiance to Time, though he had toyed with her abundant tresses, as the few silver threads among them showed. She had that exquisite grace and natural abandon, that harmony and flexibility of limb and figure which only comes from the pure air, nourishing and beautifying sunshine, and luxurious unrestraint of a Southern country girlhood. Upon her arrival a few weeks before she had affiliated with us as naturally as we with each other. Since that time even Effie had been a lesser luminary. She seemed as young as the youngest, was as gay as the gayest, and yet was clothed upon with an unconscious quiet dignity which bespoke the roundness and completeness of a ripened womanhood. In a week she had conquered all. Every girl had confided her sorrows and heart-aches to this new friend, and been soothed she knew not how. The dowagers were full of her praise despite themselves, and even the poor invalids seemed to gather new life from her abounding vitality, while the spiritless masculines, who were either too weak or too cowardly to compete for the prize of love and beauty in the parlors of the Northern cities, and had come to this "Castle of Indolence," in the hope that mere *ennui* might give them the *entrée* to some witless maiden's heart, found life enough to crowd our parlors at evening, and become almost endurable, under the pervading charm of her presence.

Who was she? Nobody knew, yet nobody inquired. She was Mrs. Dewar. That much the hotel register told us. It gave, too, an unknown country-seat in an upland county of the Carolinas as her home. She herself told us—not in words —that she was a lady—experienced, cultured, and surpassingly lovable. Of her domestic relations, home, past, or present life, we knew no more after three weeks of daily contact than when she first entered our circle.

On this St. Valentine's morning who does not know what was the theme of our conversation in

this girl-club, this Sorosis of the Southern hotel
veranda? If there is any one so dull, let him remain in darkness. I, at least, will not enlighten
him. In the midst of our glee Mrs. Dewar joined
us, and, sitting down upon the lounge, took Effie's
head on her lap and bedewed it with loving
caresses as she listened to our chatter. If she
loved Effie better than the rest it only added to
our admiration for her. She was unusually silent
this morning, yet I thought I had never seen her
face so radiant with joy. After a time she said
in a low mellow tone, as full of rapture as the
melody of far-off wedding-bells:

"Ah, girls! I hope the gentle saint may bring
to every one of your hearts as much of joy as he
has given to me."

There was no avoiding it then. No heart could
have resisted the entreaties of that dozen of ex-
pectant girls hungry for a romance. Lounging in
all sorts of careless attitudes upon floor, chairs, and
cushions, in bright *négligée* costumes, in the soft
spring sunshine, we listened to the story of our
unconscious enchantress.

CHAPTER II.

PAUL and I grew up as boy and girl together on adjoining plantations. He was a Dewar and I a Moyer, both old families that reached back into the chaos of colonial times with certainty, and had a fund of traditionary lore which made no account of centuries and was daring enough to claim the best blood in more than one kingdom for its origin. Of course we never tested this theory, and it might have been apocryphal. I suspect we all thought it to be, but we were beyond denial among the first families of the Carolinas, and it was a pleasant and harmless amusement to speculate upon what our ancestors might have been before the establishment of the De Grafenreidt's colony of Swiss and Palatine at the junction of the Neuse and Trent. Of course they had constituted a part of that colony. The proof of that was incontestable; yet Paul used to say it would be hard to satisfy a jury even of that. But he was always a doubter. His mother was a

Boutright, who, though as good a woman as ever lived, had no family to speak of. I think it was his perfect adoration of his mother that made Paul delight particularly in ridiculing our old family notions.

We always called each other "cousin," though we never could discover that we were any kin to each other. We were slightly connected by collateral marriages, but I do not think there had ever been any intermarriage between our families, unless it was in the old days before they came to America.

As I said, though, we had been boy and girl together; our plantation was just above theirs on the river. His father was also the testamentary guardian of the estate devised to me by my father, who had died in my infancy. He was an only son and I an only daughter. Both houses had been almost equally homes to both of us. Even in childhood I had spent months at a time at my guardian's, and when we grew older Paul's mother always complained that his vacations were spent at Hickory Grove, our home, instead of Oakland, his father's place.

We fished, rode, hunted, sung, read, laughed, and would have cried together had there been any occasion for tears in our young lives. I cannot remember when I did not love him with a jealous passionateness, and he had protected and cared for me so long that we were accounted lovers almost before we had ceased to be children. Yet we had hardly interchanged a word of love in our lives. Our affection had been open and undisguised from childhood, but we had never talked about it. We could not remember when caresses and endearments were not as much a matter of course between us as if I had been his sister. I should have been amazed if he had not greeted me every day when we first met with a kiss; and once when I refused him my lips when he had just come home after a long absence at college, I think he thought I had parted with my wits. I doubt if he knows to-day that it was simply a piece of innocent coquetry, designed to heighten the pleasure of yielding. It was provoking, the way he acted about it, too. He never attempted to put aside my hands or overcome my feigned aversion either by violence or persuasion, and I had to steal behind him as he leaned back in the great arm-chair upon the porch that evening and kiss his newly-bearded lips, or I verily believe I should not have known their touch until to-day.

Our betrothal had been as much a matter of course as our courtship. It was a right romantic one, too. I had never worn a ring. The truth is, I was vain of my hand : it was counted very shapely in those days. I had always said that I would never wear any ring but one solitaire and one plain gold—meaning, of course, an engagement and a wedding ring. It was a mere piece of vanity, as I wished to make my hands noticeable by the absence of these usual adornments ; a resolution to which I have strictly adhered," she added, as she glanced at a plain gold circlet and a diamond solitaire which adorned her exquisite hand.

One day Paul took my hand in his great palm and said, half musingly :

"You ought to have a ring, Cousin Sue."

"You know well enough, sir, the reason why I have none," I said mockingly, with never a thought that I was challenging him to woo me, though I was ready to marry him that instant if he had but asked me to do so. He smiled in his grave way and said :

" Do you adhere to your old fancy about rings ?"

I saw then what a forward hoyden I had been, and was angry at myself for having done so, and at him for taking advantage of my unmeaning banter, as I thought he must have known it was. I felt my face grow hot, and as I jerked away my hand and flashed a look up at his face, I saw he was smiling down at my embarrassment. I was right down angry then, and determined that I would carry it through with as brazen a face as I thought he had tried to put upon me, so I snapped out:

"Yes, I do, sir!" and making him a low, mock courtesy, I left the porch and went off to my room to cry for shame or anger—I hardly knew which. It was the first mean thing I had ever known of Paul Dewar.

When he came the next day, I was half a mind to run away; but before I could decide whether to go or stay he had come into the sitting-room where I was with mamma, who was not well then, and before I knew it, almost, had kissed us both, as he had done every time he had come for so many years, and was sitting in the sunshine before mother's sofa, with his head in her lap, like a great boy as he was, while she stroked his brown locks which the sunlight transformed into a golden crown upon his brow. Then he read to us and laughed and chatted until I forgot the escapade

of the day before, and was as contented as if I
had never made that unmaidenly speech, which I
began to think he did not notice after all. I was
hemming some handkerchiefs for him and working a pretty monogram of his initials in the corner
at that very time.   Finally he took a little leather
case from his pocket, opened it, and held it
towards me.   It contained a plain gold ring and a
diamond solitaire.

"Which will you have, Cousin Sue?" he asked
in his provoking, calm way.   I was angry that he
should pursue the cruel jest, which my thought-
lessness had allowed him to make at my expense,
instead of asking me nicely, as a lover should, to
be his wife; so I said, coolly:

"Suppose I don't choose either, sir?" and handed the case back to him.   My mother seemed to
have just comprehended the scene, or all of it except the color it obtained from our previous conversation, and began to laugh.   Paul took the
case and said quietly:

"Very well.   They are both yours whenever
you choose."

Then mother asked to see them, looked at
them carefully and then at me, and said significantly:

" You do not know what you are throwing away."

I could not stand that, but jumped up and ran to my room to have another cry.

Paul stayed, and I heard him talking with mamma a long time. Finally I stole out of the house and went along the path I knew he would take in going home until I came to a grapevine which clambered up to daylight and sunshine over the bolls and branches of a grove of oaks and hickorys. It was just in blossom then, and the subtle fragments of the little clustering flowers filled the whole grove as if it were carpeted with mignonette. I sat down upon one of the long, pendent vines and swung myself back and forth nursing my wrath.

Presently along came Paul whistling as carelessly as if I had never lived. How cold and mean it seemed!

" Ha! Cousin Sue," he cried as he came opposite where I was. "You here?"

" O Cousin Paul!" I burst out, and the tears would come in spite of me. " How could you be so mean! And right before mamma, too! You know I am willing to wear your ring," I sobbed; " that is—if—if you want I should."

"What in the world would I offer it to you for unless I wished you to wear it? There, there, never mind, dear," patting my head as if I were a fretted child; "there, take your choice," said he, holding the box towards me, "either one, or both."

I took out the engagement ring and laid it in my hand.

"Won't you have the other, too?" he asked.

Did you ever hear of such impertinence? But I was determined he should not make me angry again, so I merely said:

"No, I thank you, not at present."

What do you suppose he did? Just shut up the case and put it in his vest pocket, with:

"Very well. It is all ready whenever you *do* want it."

Was there ever such an oaf at love-making? I could have cried again, but would not. So I sat rocking back and forth in the grapevine swing with the ring still lying in the palm of my hand.

"Why don't you put it on?" he asked.

"No, Cousin Paul," I said, and I think there must have been an undertone of triumph in my voice, for I saw my time had come at last, "that would never do. You must put it on with a kiss and a rhyme, or it will be unlucky."

" Pshaw," he said fretfully, " what do you want to bother me for?"

" Bother you?" I asked innocently. " Nothing of the kind ; but I will never invite bad luck by putting it on myself."

He knew I would not ; so after much tribulation he made a rhyme, whispered it in my ear, slipped the ring upon my finger and kissed my lips—the dear old bear—quite lover-like.

CHAPTER III.

"A WORD IN SEASON—HOW GOOD IT IS!"

AND that was all his lovemaking. He just
kept coming and going as he had always
done, never giving me another pretty word or a
tenderer caress, calling me "Cousin Sue" as he
had before, and just being the same dear kind
Paul whom I had always loved to distraction. I
put on all the little artful ways I could invent to
induce him to play the lover, but he would not.
He would be just plain Paul and I his cousin
Sue.

So you may well imagine how surprised I was,
when the next anniversary of the lover's saint
came round, to receive a valentine from my staid,
matter-of-course, lover-cousin Paul. Although
we were known to be engaged and had been
counted the same as betrothed for many a year, I
was still something of a belle in the country, and
Valentine's day never passed without my receiving my full share of flattering and amatory
epistles through the post. I had never had one

from Paul, however, and had never dreamed of his being guilty of such commonplace frivolity.

I had started Peter, the house boy, right early that morning to the post-office a mile away, and when he came back there it was with the others —just a plain white envelope among the many quaint and elegant devices which others had sent me. There was no cupid or torch or loving legend visible upon it, but simply the honest manly superscription,

"MISS SUSIE MOYER,
Mamelon."

No one would have dreamed it to have been anything pertaining to love or St. Valentine's day. It looked like an ordinary every-day letter; and as I did not happen to notice that the superscription was Paul's it was left unopened until all its more pretentious companions had been opened, read, and commented upon by mamma, who, dear, delicate, loving creature, was almost as much interested in my pleasures as I was myself. She had been a widow and in somewhat delicate health so long that I had become more of an associate than daughters usually are to a mother. Besides, she was not yet old. She had married young and I was her oldest and only child. Then, too, she was one of those women whose hearts never can grow old. I can see her now as she sat that morning in her elegant wrap, with the waving steely-gray hair lying above her broad, low brow, her great dark eyes full of a soft tender light as she watched my eager vivacity and reached out her slender white hand for every epistle that had amused or interested me—praising those that were tasteful, admiring the quaint and costly, and laughing her own low, gurgling, mellow laugh over those that were humorous or grotesque.

She had never said a word to me about my engagement with Paul—had never even made a remark about the ring I wore—but a thousand times I had seen her eager looks rest upon us with untold tenderness when we were together; and I had never in my playful moods been un- usually demonstrative towards him in her pres- ence that I did not catch her eye watching in approbation. Paul had been her favorite always; from a lubberly boy to a great awkward man she had always petted him, and he had been much more of a gallant to her than to me. My dear,

pretty mamma! How many fine speeches I had
heard him make to her while he had not one for
me. Sometimes I was half jealous of her, as
indeed I should have wholly been if I had not
known that she loved me so well that she could
love no one else better. So I knew that she
loved Paul only less than I did, and would be
supremely happy whenever she could call us both
her children in truth, as she had done in sport
for so many years. I believe I thought almost
as much of our dear mamma's delight in thinking
of our marriage as of my own.

When I had read all the others I picked up the
white envelope which lay at the bottom and saw
that it was directed in Paul's hand. How guilty I
felt as I opened it, that I had let the great, glaring
trash hide this jewel from my eyes! It was only
a few unpretentious verses signed with his own
name by my "true Valentine," indeed. I can
never forget a word of those lines, but no one
else would consider them remarkable—at least,
no one who did not know and love my Paul.

I could not help weeping as I read them from
very joy, and could only answer my mother's surprised,

"Why, Susie, what is the matter?" by handing

the sheet to her and burying my face in her lap
as she read.

Then we laughed and cried together over the
rough halting lines and agreed that he ought not
to be required to serve longer for his Rachel
We were old enough: I was twenty and Paul
twenty-three, and both had ample estates. Besides, mamma was afraid that her heart-disease
might carry her off and she should miss seeing
our joy.

"Of course," she said, "I should not feel as if I
were leaving you unprotected, for I know how
strong and true Paul is; but you do not know,
darling, how I long to see with my own eyes your
union.

So we two loving women agreed together that
my lover should be rewarded for the tender
words of his first valentine by having the period
of probation shortened and an early day named
for our wedding.

He came himself in the evening. I met him
at the door, saluted him with mock solemnity,
ushered him into the sitting-room, and presented
him to mamma as "Sir Valentine, of Oakland
Villa!"

He bore his honors meekly and asked me to go

and ride with him, for the weather was as balmy
almost as May. Oh! how happy I was during
that long canter! I was sure he would ask me to
wear the other ring soon, and then I would give
him his reward for his patient waiting and his
words of manly love and tenderness in that sweet
valentine. I had hid it in my bosom, and my
heart seemed to throb with joy beneath its pressure. But the ride ended and the night came,
and he had not asked me. I was provoked that
he would not see how I longed for him to speak.
I sang and played for him, and soon mamma
pleaded weakness for once without cause, that we
might be left alone. Then I plied all my reserved
batteries of charms, but he would not yield. He
was kind and tender. I could see the love light
dancing in his blue eyes, but he was silent as the
Sphinx upon the one subject which engaged all
my thoughts. At length, while he sat holding
my hand in both of his, I said innocently enough:

"Don't you think, Cousin Paul, that I ought to
have another ring?"

"Certainly," he said, as coolly as if it were a
matter of every-day occurrence, "I have the
other here;" and he drew the case from his
pocket, took out the ring and held it between his

thumb and finger. Then he took my hand as if he would put it on.

"What!" I exclaimed, withdrawing my hand, "You are not going to put it on *now*, are you?"

"Yes, why not?"

"Why not, certainly!" said I, very much disappointed at his cool reception of the favor I had granted him. "It *might* be well to try it on."

I laughed nervously in my vexation. I could have cried from bitter disappointment. I knew he loved me, but he would not say so. I could not think he meant to pain me, but I was so sick for love—for a sign of love. If he would only love me—only show his love—say I was dear to him! So I held up my hand for him to try on my wedding-ring with my heart full of sorrow and wounded love.

"Which finger shall I put it on?" he asked.

"Why *this* one," I answered pettishly, "as if you did not *know* on which finger a *wedding*-ring was worn!"

"Why, Cousin Sue! you don't mean—?"

I thought he would faint for an instant, then the great, strong arms were wrapped around me, and I was folded to his heart, while kisses rained on lips and cheeks and brow and hair—a blissful shower of lovedrops—till even my hungry heart was sated.

Would you believe me, girls, the stupid fellow did not know that I loved him at all.

He had heard me say that I would never wear but two rings, a plain gold and a solitaire, and never thought of their significance. So I had done all the wooing at last. I would have been angry if I had not loved him so.

It was too late then to waste any time in regrets if indeed I had been inclined to. If my lover had been slow in his wooing, he was eager enough to make amends now.

So when May came, with her lap full of roses, Paul and I were married, and I was the envy of many a fair girl in the country round, who came to see us united. If I was proud of myself, my husband, my home and all that surrounded our bridal, it was not to be wondered at. It did seem as if every circumstance which could tend to enhance our happiness had conspired with every other joyful event to crown our nuptials with good omen. Two broad plantations, lying side by side upon the splashing Dan; the broad bottoms, rich with unnumbered harvests; the rolling uplands, crowned here and there with tobacco-barns, grim and unsightly, but suggestive of a wealth of golden aromatic leaf which few sections could rival and none excel. Few would be wealthier than we, between the mountains, whose shadowy forms hung soft and misty in our western horizon, and the sea, whose steady breezes came to us in summer across the eastern lowlands. Two old families, closely connected but not of kin, would be united; and two households already so closely joined that a new element in either must have disturbed both, would be still more closely linked by the marriage of an only son and an only daughter. If there was an element of happiness which was not found in our nuptials, no one knew it then. I verily believe there was but one, and that, alas! I did not know for many years afterwards. We had been playmates and friends so long, yet I little understood what a heart was being bound to mine by the responses in the marriage service.

Our marriage made little difference with our lives. They had been unconsciously united for many years. Before that Paul had lived at Oakland and visited Hickory Grove daily; now he lived at Hickory Grove and visited Oakland daily —that was all. Yet both were homes to us. We had no care, for Paul's father attended to both estates and would have been much affronted had his son offered to relieve him of any portion of his labors. It was a strange life we led. To our parents we were still children. They would not let us be anything else, and I do not think we were anxious to dispel the illusion which those fond hearts, who had made us their idols for so many years, still threw about our lives. They took the burden of our future upon themselves and left us to bask in the sunshine of the present.

We took no bridal tour, because, Paul said, it would be too bad to deprive these dear ones at home of the sight of our pleasure. So our lives went on unbrokenly, and to each other and our parents we were still " Cousin Paul " and " Cousin Sue," as we had been before.

CHAPTER IV.

I T must not be supposed, however, that we
were idle; at least, Paul was not.

All up and down our river were the footprints
of an extinct race. Our beautiful valley was
studded with the relics of an age and race forgotten, unknown, unnamed. Here in some far-
away time seemed to have been the seat of
empire of a race of beings unlike any other races
or tribes who have lived within the ken of history, in their habits of life and action, surrounded
by circumstances developing powers and necessi-
tating a manner of life, which no human knowledge of to-day can parallel or unravel—a people
displaying only the arts of the savage, yet erect-
ing monuments whose durability and extent are
the wonders of civilization. Flint arrow-heads,
hammers, and pottery cut from the solid rock are
washed out by the river-freshets and turned up
by the plowshare, in the bottom-lands, year after
year. In those old days the valleys must have

teemed with myriads of this nameless race. Here they lived and fought and wrought, and from hence they disappeared before the forests grew or the Indians chose their hunting grounds.

The corn grows rank and high in the bottoms year by year, feeding its freshness on the mol. dering antediluvians. Curiously enough, I have even seen the fibrous maize-roots crowding the openings of a skull from which some famous artisan's or warrior's eyes may have looked forth; or filling the cavity in which some sage's brain may have throbbed before tradition found a tongue or history began to count the ages. Chief among these relics were several mounds found here and there along the river, and first among these in perfection of form and preservation was one scarcely a bowshot from my mother's home. It stood upon the edge of the second bottoms, thirty or forty yards across and as many feet in height; in form a rounded sugar-loaf, and bearing in its very center an oak which was accounted the monarch of the forest for miles around, even in that region of wide-branching oaks. The summit and slope had been smoothed and seeded by my father, and some smaller trees had been encouraged to attempt a growth in the shade of the great oak. Some rude benches had been placed about the foot of the tree, and a rustic staircase led to a quaint summer-house which was built upon the lower branches and around the trunk of the great oak. Tended with care for many years, this mound had become an island of leafy green amid the sea of grain which in the summer swelled in golden billows across the valley to the river's edge, and had been a favorite resort for Paul and myself from childhood. We called it Mamelon—a name by which it had been known for many generations in the country round.

Paul had always been terribly curious about these mounds, and especially about our Mamelon. He had measured, estimated and speculated about it for years. Who built it? when and for what purpose? seemed to be questions which rose up in his mind whenever he saw its green sloping sides or oak-crowned summit.

Long before our marriage he had taken up an idea that he would know all that could be learned of that strange people, who had dwelt upon our soil so many years ago that none knew when they lived, whence they came, nor how or why they disappeared. So he gathered books and specimens of their handiwork, arrow-heads, hammers, and spears, and the curious disks with which he thought they played some game of chance or skill; he opened some of the mounds along the river bank, cutting through them with great care, noting the position of everything, finding kettles and pipes and skeletons in all manner of positions and in all degrees of perfectness. So that Hickory Grove soon became a museum of antiquities, and one wing of it an involuntary mausoleum of several distressed-looking specimens of the mound-builders, who had been carefully taken from the places that had known them so long, and hung in articulated grandeur, each in his own individual box. So Paul became a man of science, and was just as patient and earnest in collecting these curious things, and in making surmises from them, as other men are in what they term business.

I must confess I liked it too. Not that I would not have been glad if he had been inclined to what we call a more active life. I thought there was so much strength and manhood about my giantly Great-heart, that it pained me right often to think that the great busy world was going on and paying no heed to his life or thought. There was no need for him to labor, but I wanted the world to feel his power. I was half sorry that he was not at the bar and would take no part in politics. It seemed to me that this work which he had chosen was only fit for his idle hours, his recreation, and not grand enough to be the sober business of his life.

It was pleasant, though, to go with him and note how earnestly he worked, and how, even in these sports of his mind, he was so much stronger than others. How often I noted his shrewd guesses at the lives and habits of those old-time dwellers on our river bank, and wondered whether my Paul would never come nearer to the present, never do anything grander or more practical, than guess how many generations it took to pierce a flinty hammer-head, or what was the use to which this vanished race had put a cuboid *discus*. It consoled me somewhat that he knew more of these things than anybody else; and I was proud enough when distinguished strangers came to consult him, to witness his excavations, to learn and wonder at what he knew of this self-buried and long-forgotten people. I was proud when I saw his name in magazines and read the articles which his busy pen produced, and was glad to aid him by making drawings of whatever implement, bone, or relic he desired, to illustrate his writings. I was not, though, so greatly devoted to the end he had in view. His explorations smacked too much of the charnel house for me, but I delighted to be with him, and wandering about the fields and woods was but a continuation of the sweet boy-and-girl life of our unmarried days. His "hobby," as I called it, furnished occupation for thought and a pretense for long rambles, without care and only the healthful fatigue which abundant exercise in air and sunshine brings. I counted it play. I was half sorry that my giant would waste his grand strength in mere curious research; but if he would, I was glad that he had chosen one so innocent and healthful that I could join him in it and be ever at his side.

The predictions with which our married life began continued to be made in regard to it. All my friends thought my husband a model, and it was a matter of general remark that we were the most thoroughly satisfied couple in the world, as it was admitted we had abundant reason to be.

I never could get thoroughly interested in his relics, though; and to amuse myself I began to pick up and arrange in his cabinet the pretty and curious stones which I found in our long rambles. I had never studied geology, and did not do this from any love of science or from any regard for the rocks themselves, but just to relieve the ghostly array of yellowish-brown bones and skulls and relics of the tombs upon my husband's shelves.

Sometimes my Mentor would discourse to me upon some fragment of rock I had picked up during the day, and though I lacked application to study and speculate as he did, I came unconsciously to have considerable interest in a past so remote that the one in which *he* was absorbed seemed but as yesterday in comparison with it. So it came about after a time that there was an unclassified geological museum mixed up with the carefully arranged and labeled archæological curiosities at Hickory Grove. Paul used to intimate sometimes that I ought to study these things, saying that I had a taste for geology. But I thought one scientist in the family was enough, and I loved much better to watch him at his work and let my thoughts play truant in the past which might have been, than vex my poor brain to decide what it was. My pictured stones, odd crystals, and quaintly worn pebbles were pretty enough to me, without trying to puzzle out how they became so. Men are so curious! They can never be content to enjoy things as they find them. They must know how they were made, and why; whether there are any more such, and where; and perhaps will end by trying to find or make or conceive something better or rarer. Women are called curious, too; but they have not half the curiosity of the sterner sex. I did not care what these things had been, and when Paul tried to make me study them in a quiet way, by lecturing me on every pebble I picked up, I quit gathering them, or did it only by stealth—to avoid being shown to be such an ignorant dummy as his lectures always made me think I was. *He* was so wise that I did not care to be any wiser, but did not like to have him think how little I knew when compared with him.

I do not think he would ever have dared to profane our beautiful home-mound—dear, leafy, green-carpeted Mamelon—if the elements had not been in league with his desires. But when the lightning had blasted our oak and scattered our pretty rustic house, we knew—mamma and I —that the mound was fated. Paul had ex- hausted everything else far and near. We knew he would not invade it unless we should consent, and we knew, too, that we could never withstand his entreaties. So we made a virtue of necessity, and mamma asked him one day why he did not make an excavation in Mamelon, pretending—artful woman—that it would interest her greatly to see those quaint relics of a wonderful past taken from their original resting-place. One would have thought she was never so curious about anything as the origin and purpose of that mound and the race and habits of its builders—and I chimed in with a timely amen at every pause in her conversation. What inveterate deceivers we women are! I have no idea that mamma—the sweet darling!—had ever dreamed that the mound was made for anything except evening reveries and moonlight flirtations until our irrepressible Paul began to fill his head and the house, and, as a consequence, our hearts, with relics of the mound-builders. Of course he needed no second invitation. Poor Mamelon was speedily cut and tunneled and scarred into scientific unsightliness. But, oh! what treasures he found within! Day after day the relics poured into the museum, and Paul's face shone unceasingly with the rapture of discovery. In his joy we two silly women were more than paid for our loss.

Thus the months grew into years, and Paul's thoughts seemed to have all centered on the antediluvians and their works. Our lives floated along as peacefully as the hours of a summer's day, only I could not help a sort of dissatisfaction at his backward tendencies. In a way I was ambitious; and it always hurt me to think of his leaving the bright, glorious present to delve in the forgotten past.

CHAPTER V.

"THE MINSTREL BOY TO THE WARS IS GONE."

AT length there occurred something which took my husband's attention even from the scientific pursuits in which he had been so absorbed. There began to be a talk of war. I could not help being somewhat amused, as well as wholly surprised, when I first saw my delving husband turn from the past on which he had been so intent to the present which had been sweeping unheeded by him. He was in earnest, though. Paul never played at anything. When he gave himself up to Secession he forgot the Mound Builders entirely. He thought only of what he did, and did only what he thought about.

So the winter slipped away, and almost for the first time in our lives, we were separated in our thoughts and work. He was busy and absorbed in the interests of that country whose existence he seemed but just then to have discovered, and he went back and forth with a serious, preoccupied air, being very little at home. I was much surprised and by no means displeased when he came to me one day in the spring, clad in uniform. I did not anticipate danger nor disaster. I thought there might be some fighting. Of course there could hardly be any war without it, but *he* would not be harmed, and I felt that he was where he ought to be—among men. He would be felt, appreciated and prized, I thought, in that relation. He was a colonel, he told me. I hardly knew the difference between colonel and sergeant then. I am sure I thought a captain outranked them both. I expected that he would show himself a hero, and that men would know of what my Paul was capable. It was not very patriotic, but I thought more of Paul than of the country. It may not have been so with other wives and sweethearts. They said it was not, I know, but somehow I never quite believed them. Anyhow, with me, it was Paul first and the country afterwards, and a good while afterwards, too

Well, he went away and the war came,—the terrible war which was so different from what my fancy had pictured it,—so full of suffering and horror and so fearfully long! It seemed to my poor, waiting, weary heart that it would never end! No, I was not brave. I did not want it to go on. I could not use those fierce, boastful words which I so often heard from other fair lips. When others talked of the " last man and the last dollar," my poor, weak heart would only hear the " last dollar," and I said amen to that right gladly. I would have given up the last dollar and the last hope of the brave, bright country we thought we were building for ourselves and our children in the fair South, to have had my Paul back in my arms and safe from the dangers of those horrible battles, the wearisome marches and noisome camps—oh! I know I was not patriotic! I was just a poor, weak woman, who loved her Paul— selfishly and foolishly, no doubt—and cared for little else.

The days and weeks and months dragged wearily into years, and still the struggle waxed and waned, and the moments were burdened with an ever-increasing weight of woe.

I do not mean to tell you in detail of all the suffering and sorrow that it brought to me. I suppose every heart that felt the scath of war thought its own burden heavier than any other knew. I had certainly my share of suffering. I knew then, but somehow I could not realize it—my heart would not acknowledge it—that my lot was so comparatively fortunate that I ought rather to rejoice than murmur. My husband was wounded more than once, it is true, but not so seriously as to imperil his life, and he was winning place and honor among men daily. I have a scrap-book now which is full of what was said and written about him and his command. Of course I was proud of him and of his success and gallantry, yet somehow, —I am almost ashamed to confess it, but it is true —I was sorry that the quiet old days of the Mound Builders were passed. I used to go into the cabinet and dust and rearrange the skulls and bones, see that the labels did not become loosened or lost, read what my husband had written, and fancy that he was once more with me and engaged in our old peaceful pursuits. I had been ambitious and discontented in those old days, yet I sighed to have them back again instead of the turmoil and terrors of war, despite the glory and honor it had brought to my Paul. I knew I was weak and contradictory in my feelings and I never claimed to be otherwise.

The war itself was so distant that it did not disturb our home; yet there had been changes there. A blue-eyed boy came to my arms in the first, and Paul's father was among those that slept in the third, year of the struggle. It seemed hard for us three women then to get along upon the plantations alone. It is true we had over-seers, and it might seem that little of the care would fall on us. Alas, it was only a difference between doing directly and indirectly. Is there not an old Latin inquiry which runs something in this wise, *Quis custodiet custodes?* I thought we might have guessed that riddle then. I was foolish; but I allowed these little troubles to worry me greatly.

I had thought little of the results of the war. I had little fear in regard to them. I knew our fortunes were desperate; but I had so much confidence in Paul that I could not believe he would fail. I think I had a sort of dull, blind faith that the Confederacy would succeed, and an expectation that its success would be mainly due to my Paul. I wonder if I was the only woman in all the South who had such foolish dreams. Yet, I did not think so much of this. I wanted the war to end, in order that I might have Paul at home again. I did not once think what we would be, or how situated, if we should fail.

At length the spring came once more, and the

very air seemed full of forebodings. Rumors of
strife and defeat came daily and hourly. All
waited for the end which a universal prescience
indicated to be close at hand. Few made any
preparations to "pitch a crop," under the apprehension that Yankees would harvest it if they
did.

So the days went by until at length there came
along the roads, from the northward, scattering
soldiers, with dejected looks, weary and worn,
with sad, disheartened tales of battle and defeat.
They had given up, and were going to their
homes, convinced that all was lost. Of the fate
of those who had stayed behind they could give
no hint—or not more than a hint, at least. Gradually these scattered units grew into a straggling,
disintegrated host, and the South Side, Peters-
burg, and at length Appomattox, became sounds
of overwhelming but familiar horror. We knew,
we realized then, that all was lost! Lee had
failed! The Army of Virginia was broken,
routed! The end had come! Then I knew tnat
somewhere among the *débris* of a scattered nation
was my Paul, alive or dead, broken or whole—I
knew not! For the first time, then, I believe, I
fully felt what war was, and wondered that I

could have been so careful and anxious about a thousand trivialities while its terrible facts were being wrought out around me by those I knew and loved.

This terrible apprehension, however, thank God! was but brief in its duration. In the gray twilight, as I sat before the fire in the old sitting-room, I heard the tramp of a horse upon the lawn and the whinney of old Bob, the thoroughbred, whom Paul had ridden away four years before. I knew it, and in an instant was out of the room, across the porch, and down the steps. A drooping figure was dismounting from the faithful horse, whose strength had scarcely been sufficient to bring his master home. How I clasped the sinking, dusty figure, with kisses and tears and hysteric laughter, it would be weak to tell. I dragged him into the sitting-room at once, and had off his worn and soiled uniform, with its general's stars upon the collar, and all that the house afforded of cheer and comfort was brought to make my Paul welcome home. Yet all did not bring a smile to his face. He had kissed me absently when I first went out, and had given a cold embrace to mamma when he came in; but he did not seem to realize that he was at home. I prattled and bustled about, but could bring no warmth to his voice or eyes. Finally, I brought the little son, whom he had never seen, and put him in his father's arms. Then the hopeless, horrible stolidity went out of Paul's face, and a flash of intensest anguish succeeded it, as he said :

"Do you know, darling, that we are ruined, that all—all is lost?"

He put his hands over his face, groans and sobs convulsed his frame, and tears fell upon the wondering, upturned face of his boy. I had never seen Paul manifest any emotion before, and I was terrified at the intensity of his grief. I stood for a moment, stunned at what I saw, and then cast my arms about his neck, saying impulsively :

"O Paul, you have *me !*"

My heart was saying, "I have *you*," and it was little I cared for the cause that was lost, now that my Paul had returned safe to my arms. Of course I could not speak so slightingly of what moved him so deeply, and, not knowing what I could *say* to comfort him, I only offered him my weak, silly self.

It seemed to touch him though, for he put

down the boy, clasped me in his arms and kissed me tenderly on the lips as he said:

"Yes, indeed, I have you, and you alone, to live for now."

I had never dreamed that his soul was so wrapped up in the cause he had served.

CHAPTER VI.

"POORTITH'S PORTION CAULD."

IT had never occurred to me, in my dreaming, that when the war should end we could not go back to the old life, until I saw how utterly it had obliterated all that went before from the memory and heart of Paul. He had given himself unreservedly to the Confederate cause; for four years he had had no thought of which it was not an essential ingredient, and he had twined his future with its fate so inseparably in all his plans and schemes that he could not now bring himself to consider a future in which it had no place. I had regretted once that he had so little ambition, and when I saw now how completely ambition had occupied the chambers of his heart I could not but feel punished for my former discontent. He seemed to have lost all interest in the future and to have forgotten that there was any past save that brief interval when the "stars and bars" floated above their unfaltering defenders. He

brooded forever over their defeat, and could see
no hope nor light in the future. He shrank from
his fellows and seemed imbued with a morbid
dread of the turmoil and bustle of business. He
seemed to look forward to no future for himself
or his children. More than all he seemed to take
no delight in my presence and to care nothing for
my wishes. At least so it appeared to me. It is
true, he never tired of gazing at me, and would
sit for hours with his sad brooding eyes following my every motion, but he would not enter into
any of my plans or take any interest in what I
proposed to do. His old joking, bantering ways
were gone. He never even made pleasant blund-
ers now.

It hurt me terribly at first to think that I had
lost all power to console or cheer, and gradually
my grief turned to anger. I thought he was so
selfish and heartless to dodge the cares and re-
sponsibilities of the future because he had been involved in one great failure. I thought it could be
no harder for him—a great strong man, who had
shown himself able to pluck honor and fame from
the very brow of defeat—than for me, a weak helpless woman. I did not consider how a man loves
as his own child a nation he has helped to create.

I even became very angry—God pity me that I was so blind—that he should give way to misfortune and waste his life in vain regrets for an irretrievable past.

So I grew cold and hard towards him; our lives swung away from each other, and while yet under the old roof-tree we were separated a thousand times farther than when he was in the army. I never knew how it came about, but I began to regard Paul with something of contempt, and to think of him as an insignificant figure in that future which must be met by every one. I did not hate him, perhaps I even loved him more tenderly than ever, but I thought of him as one who had needlessly deserted from the battle of life. All the pride I had in him before went out, and I only regarded him as a weak and kindly failure, a hopeless victim of hypochondria.

It is true there was abundant reason for desponding. Those who were not present to view the struggle which confronted the people of the South after the war can hardly understand it. Not only was all our slave property gone, but all debts builded on the faith of such property were generally valueless. The fact that a new system

of labor must be relied on to make the lands pro-
ductive exerted so depressing an influence that
thousands of plantations went for a song. Those
who were rich before, who had never dreamed
that they would ever be required to labor for a
support, were glad of an opportunity to do so.
Stock to work with was scarce, labor uncontroll-
able and the future uncertain. Under these
circumstances perhaps any one who had been
always accustomed to luxury and ease might
well have despaired. But this was not all in our
case.

The estate of Paul's father had not been settled.
Paul had himself appointed administrator as soon
as the courts were open, and began an examination
of the affairs of the estate, I think with the hope
of finding something which might improve our
fortunes. Alas, he was doomed to bitter disappointment. The estate of Wilson Dewar aside
from his plantation had been accounted in ante-
war days considerable. At the beginning of the
war he had owned several hundred slaves, and was
considered to have been worth more than a hundred thousand dollars. Here is the schedule
which Paul made out after a long and patient in-
vestigation of his father's affairs, after laying off

what is termed a "year's support for the widow,"
his mother,—it is old and worn, but legible :

Available Assets:

1740 acres of land with life estate of widow on one third, say	$17,400
Proceeds of sale of personality	1,200
Old bank bills, worth about 6 cents on a dollar	1,000
Solvent credits	2,500
	$22,100

Unavailable Assets:

One barrel full of Confederate money and bonds and State securities tainted with rebellion	75,000
Bills of sale of 212 slaves liberated by Lincoln's proclamation	150,000
Individual notes and bonds rendered worthless by the results of the war	40,000
	$265,000

Total known liabilities	74,000
Unproved old debts, probably	6,000
	$80,000

"In other words, Sue," he said bitterly, when
he had shown it to me, "the estate of Wilson
Dewar will not pay twenty-five cents on the dollar, and you are married to a pauper who does
not know how to do anything to support you except fight and play gentleman. And worse than
all, Sue, your own estate, which my father held
as your guardian, has been swallowed up in the

general wreck, and you have nothing in the world now except this plantation, with nobody and nothing to work it with. My father having carried on both plantations, nearly all the stock belonged to his estate, and must be sold to pay his debts. You might better have married an overseer, Sue. He could at least have worked and made bread and meat for you."

He rose and left the house before I could say a word. I was completely astounded at what he had told me. To think that we were actually *poor;* that we had only our old home plantation, with no means of working even that, was a most overwhelming thought. We had not been accustomed to what in one of our Northern cities in these later days would be termed an extravagant mode of life. Few even of the wealthiest nabobs of slave aristocracy were inclined to anything like the display which shoddy, petroleum and stock-gambling have made familiar to us since the social deep burst its bounds and the barriers of society were swept away. [Some of us looked hard at the others as she spoke, but the little lady did not seem to know that she was hitting any of our circle, and evidently was quite unconscious of the fact that *we* might view the up-

heaval of which she spoke in an altogether different light. So no one made any remark.] We had
just lived in plain, healthy, up-country planter style,
conscious that we could have whatever of luxury
we desired, but content with our horses and family
carriage, a half dozen or so of extra servants, and
an almost entire freedom from care or responsi-
bility of any kind. Probably no aristocracy which
the world has ever seen contented itself with so
cheap, healthy and rational amusement or in-
dulged so little in enervating luxuries.

Genuine comfort and the unrestrained enjoyment of natural delights marked the tendency of
the slave aristocracy rather than mere display or
luxuries which depend on a spirit of rivalry
rather than a desire for enjoyment. Men worth
hundreds of thousands lived in houses, and drove
equipages, which a well-to-do Northern farmer
would hardly consider fit for his occupancy. No
one did anything simply to outstrip his neighbor.
There was little of envy among that class, but a
prevailing idea of comfort and an abiding indis-
position to exertion. We lived for enjoyment,
but our pleasures were simple, unostentatious,
healthful.

Therefore it was that the slave-holding aristoc-

racy of the South was so fine a race of men and
women physically. Whatever there was of dissi-
pation was cured by repose and exercise in the
open air, not violent nor under the whip and spur
of necessity, but leisurely and habitual. Excepting some families who were enfeebled by intermarriage, they were certainly the finest race, in
their physical attributes, which has resulted from
the European occupancy of American soil. The
men were large and harmoniously developed; not
worn by useless struggle with the world, nor
dwarfed by exotic culture or absorbing vices.
The ladies—well, it does not become me to say
much of them; but I have often thought, when I
compared our out-door assemblies of rosy-cheeked,
round-limbed, unrestrained, natural girls, with—
well, dears, you know I mean no disparagement;
but while Northern girls may be smarter and
brighter in a way, we do think our Southern ones
are healthier and stronger than those victims of
long winters, close rooms, tight stoves, and a
forced hot-house system of education.

But we were not well versed in the arts of self-
support. Our luxury had consisted largely in
having the burdens of life lifted from our shoulders, and we were not trained in bearing them.

A Northern family, reduced from almost any position in life, who yet had a good plantation, with health and youth still left to them, would not have felt themselves utterly prostrated. We had always had so many to do *for* us, and knew so little how to do for ourselves, that we were very nearly helpless. With the science and art of oversight we were familiar. No one can direct others with so little care and so great effect as the old-time master and mistress of the plantation. But now we had no one to direct.

Many of our former slaves would have remained with us, but we did not feel justified in hiring many since we had nothing to pay. Of course we could not feed them longer, for we looked with apprehension at the rapidly diminishing stores we had. We had made some preparations for a crop before, but it was impossible to carry out our intentions, for want of money to obtain our supplies.

It all came upon me in an instant as I sat there after Paul had gone out that day. *We were poor.* Even the overseers whom we had been wont to hire were richer in the power of self-support than we. It is true we had the plantation, but it was worth but little without the labor which had

made it profitable. It is true we could even with
our own labor raise enough to prevent actual
want, but it must be at the sacrifice of our old
lives. We must become manual workers, and
know nothing of that leisure we had loved and
enjoyed so long. Not only that, but we must
learn to labor and look only to ourselves for what
we had. It seemed a terrible loss of caste, too.
The distinction between high and low hitherto
had been compulsory labor. There is a general
idea that manual labor was accounted menial and
degrading among us. It was not that at all,—it
was the *necessity* of labor which marked the divid-
ing line. The man who was not compelled to
labor might delve unremittingly; he might, as it
were, enslave his children, making them co-laborers
with the slave without either of them losing
caste by it; but if such labor was necessary
for their support they were branded, with more
or less rigorousness according to locality, as *poor*,
and were esteemed accordingly.

That I was utterly prostrated by this thought
is not to be wondered at. I rushed to my own
room and cried all the evening, quite forgetful of
Paul and the effect of this on him. It was late
when he came in to supper, and I must have pre-

sented a disconsolate appearance as I sat behind
the great coffee-pot which had resumed its wonted
dignity at our Southern country suppers now that
the blockade was over and real coffee sent its
aroma over the board again. I wonder how
many Southern families spent the first green-
backs they ever saw for coffee. I hardly know
one who did not.

But the coffee was not good enough to keep
Paul. He gave one glance at my tear-stained face
and then went out into the darkness. I knew he
had gone on account of my demeanor, yet I felt
so discouraged and humiliated that I would not
go after him and call him back. My own misery
filled my heart so full that I could not think of
his. The supper was over and the hours crept
on, but he did not come. I sent a servant to
search for him, but he could not be found. I
hardly cared: I even blamed him for adding to
my sorrow by his conduct. He did not come
that night, and I sobbed and moaned myself to
sleep.

The next morning I learned that he had taken
his breakfast very early and had gone out on the
plantation. He did not come home at noon, but
sent to the cook for his dinner. In the evening I

went out to see why he had stayed away all day. I wandered on until I came to the new ground, and there I saw my Paul working in the tobacco side by side with the niggers,—working his old war horse Bob, who seemed to be quite contented in his degradation.

You may think I was much affected by what I saw and so I was, but not as you suppose, nor as I ought to have been. I was angry,—angry at Paul too. It seemed as if he were trying to humiliate me still further. I sat down in the bushes at the edge of the wood and cried and moaned bitterly.

Why, I thought, could he not do something else, if he must work! Why not engage in some genteel employment? He might be an Insurance Agent or a " Runner" for some mercantile house or,—or—anything else but a laborer.

I went back to the house with a sadly unjust and bitter heart. Paul came to supper that night all worn and weary, his hands blistered and both body and soul prostrated with fatigue and helplessness. I saw it, but I did not spare or cheer him. I poured out on his head the same reproaches I had conned over when I saw him toiling in the hot sun. I accused him of not loving

me and of trying to humiliate and degrade me
still further. Oh! I don't know what I did not
say to him that was mean and aggravating, but I
went too far at last. I had never seen him angry
before and I am sure I never shall again.

"Mrs. Dewar," he said,—only think of his calling me Mrs. Dewar,—"Mrs. Dewar, I am not
responsible for any of the misfortunes that have
befallen you except your marriage with me,
which you seem so much to regret. I shall
endeavor to prevent your feeling the blow which
has so humiliated you, but must take my own
way to do it."

I was so amazed that I could not speak another
word during supper, and after that was over he
went off to the wing of the house in which his
old relics were, and slept that night—and indeed
always afterwards, until a time you shall hear
about, long after ; for that foolish quarrel separated Paul's heart and mine all but forever. I was
too proud to confess that I was wrong and he had
no idea that he was in any error,—and I do not
know that he was. He could not make any
allowance for my sorrow and weakness, and I had
no idea what was in his heart.

So two years passed and we were as strangers

to each other.   Then my mother died, and for a
time it seemed as if we were going to resume our
old tender relations to each other.   But he was
too busy with his plantation work to give me the
time and attention he bestowed in the old days,
so I went back to the thought I had so long
cherished that I had come to believe its truth—
that he did not love me.   This belief had been
strengthened by the tenderness which he had all
along shown to my mother.   God forgive me, I
think I was jealous of her, even in her grave.
Her repeated solicitations that I should be recon-
ciled to Paul—her praises of him—her reproaches
of me—had all along rankled in my heart.   So I
gave myself up to my child, and he worked the
plantation by day and stayed in the old cabinet
by night.

I am ashamed to confess it, but as his hands
grew harder and he gathered the roughness and
uncouthness that accompany manual toil I began
to feel a sort of contempt, almost disgust, for
him which nearly made me cease to regret our
estrangement.   During this time however we had
prospered wonderfully, when compared with our
neighbors.   Paul had made splendid crops, had
worked a large force and received very remunera-

tive prices for what he had made. The plantation had increased in value and been greatly improved, and all the time there had been no added
care upon me. I had been lavishly supplied with
servants and had every comfort of the old life
except the sense of abundant wealth and the untold luxury of love.

I tried many times to come nearer to my husband, but he seemed so cold and absorbed that I
could not succeed. My old Paul seemed to be
dead. All that he had loved or enjoyed before
seemed to be laid aside and forgotten. He would
never speak of the war, and would get angry if
any one gave him any of the titles he had won
therein. He would be plain Paul Dewar, nothing
more, nothing less, he said, hereafter. Sometimes he would spend an hour with us in the
family room after supper, and then the careworn
anxious look would come into his eyes and he
would hurry off to his cabinet. He was always
kind to me, but never tender or demonstrative.
He had never spoken harshly to me but once, but
he was so busy that I could not make him seem
like my Paul of the old days,—so I fretted and
pined and pitied myself as if I had been a
martyr.

CHAPTER VII.

AFTER one of Paul's visits to our market town, he came home bringing with him a stranger, whom he introduced to me as "Captain Dickson." He was a man rather below the medium height, very erect in figure, with a full square head, wide mouth, heavy firm jaw, a close cropped dark beard, short hair just beginning to show a steely gray among its darkness, shaggy beetling brows with keen blue eyes beneath. I knew as soon as I saw him that he was of Northern birth, what we call a Yankee, and you may well imagine from what I have said of myself that I was not inclined to welcome him over-cordially. There was a sort of restlessness of manner, together with that unfailing look of eager watchfulness which is found in the eyes of every man who has had to struggle with the world from boyhood —a condition so usual with the Northern man that the look has become generic—an appearance of being ever on the alert, which I think has given rise to the tradition of the Yankee's keenness and shrewdness. The conflict with man and nature in the warfare of existence or with his fellows in the race for wealth and power leaves always its indelible impress on the features. Usually this was absent from the face of the Southern man of the better classes because such struggle, if it comes to him at all, comes only when he has arrived at maturity, and the features have lost their plastic and impressible character. With the Northern man of almost any grade it begins early and is unceasing. Therefore it is that our Southern idea of the Yankee is of one who sees, thinks and acts with the utmost readiness of body and mind. He is quick, stirring, restless. The idea that he is inquisitive, prying, comes less, I think, from his habit of asking questions than from his constant watchfulness. It is undoubtedly true that one of them will learn more about a family, a neighborhood or a business without asking a question than one of our people by a week's inquiry. In that I think the Yankees have been belied. I think they ought properly to be deemed the people who learn everything and ask nothing.

However that may be, Captain Dickson was a Yankee; his honest, candid, yet watchful and cau-

tious face told me that, when his eyes met mine
and measured me in an instant, before I heard or
at least comprehended Paul's explanatory com-
ment following the name of the stranger, "from
Massachusetts."

I said that I did not receive him over-cordially
—I did not mean that I had any hostility towards
him because he was a Yankee, but only a sort of
embarrassed feeling that he was of another people.
This has always been true of North and South;
they have always been two peoples. Touching in
territory, identical in language and united in gov-
ernmental forms, but distinct and separate in
habits of life and thought. I felt that Captain
Dickson was on his guard as a stranger, and I was
also on guard towards him. I did not feel that
easy cordiality which I think peculiarly marks the
demeanor of Southern people towards each other,
that ease and familiarity akin to the unrestrained
freedom of the home-circle.

However, I listened to the conversation between
him and Paul, and learned very soon that he had
come for the very purpose of exercising his peculiar Yankee gift of observation. He was looking
about to see if any unobserved end of profit might
be picked up in our quiet agricultural community.

He had an idea that some undeveloped industry might be found for which the region afforded peculiar advantages. He did not know what. He had come with no preconceived idea of what he would do, but was ready to turn to whatever might offer. He proposed to see what might be done with advantage, before he set about doing anything. He was not an educated man, in the sense we generally use that word, yet I was surprised to see how much he knew of the world's industries, and I soon saw that even Paul was no less surprised than I. He discussed the tobacco market and prospects with Paul with a breadth and sagacity of view which was amazing to us, who had been raised in constant consideration of this interest, when he told us that he had never bought, raised or owned a pound of the weed in his life. His attention being directed Southward, he had studied up its industries and had confirmed the impressions thus received by observations since. Showing him our Indian cabinet, my husband was astonished at the accurate description which he gave of some mounds which had recently been cut into by a high freshet on a neighboring river, which he had seen a few weeks before.

Every species of implement and machinery was familiar to him. He knew enough of every branch of manufacture to be willing to undertake whatever promised reasonable profit. I never learned how he came to be thrown into my husband's society, or how when once brought together they came to prove so mutually attractive. For several days he remained with us without seeming to arrive at any definite conclusion as to what he should undertake. He and Paul rode and walked and talked with an unintermitting earnestness which I could not but smile to see. At length he began to examine the timber, and they gathered pieces of oak and hickory and dogwood and persimmon, until the porch at Hickory Grove looked as if it had been transformed into a wood-shed. Then he inquired about roads and the place of shipment, the price of the raw material, and investigated very carefully the source of supply and its extent.

During all this time he said not a word of the purpose of this inquiry. We knew he was thinking of establishing some business, but we had no idea what. At length when he seemed to have fully determined on his course he said to Paul, one morning as they sat on the porch,

"Well Mr. Dewar, I have made up my mind what to do!"

"Ah! what may it be?" inquired Paul somewhat curiously.

"I shall put up an establishment somewhere in this section to turn hard woods."

"To what?" asked Paul in amazement.

"To work up these hard white woods," answered Dickson.

"I don't understand you," said Paul politely.

"I mean," said Dickson, "to make axe, pick, sledge and hammer handles, mallets, spokes, hubs and whatever else there may be a demand for, out of your hickory, persimmon and other fine woods."

"Indeed!" said my husband, and there was a tone of contempt and incredulity in his voice which I was confident would not escape the notice of his companion; nor did it.

He got up and walked once or twice across the porch before answering Paul's exclamation.

"You are mistaken, Mr. Dewar, if you think I am either jesting or a fool. Every one of these white hickory butts with which your plantation and section is studded is worth a price which would seem fabulous to you."

"What is that price?" asked Paul still incredulously.

"From ten to twenty dollars a cord," answered Dickson.

"What!" asked Paul, now thoroughly aroused. "You do not mean to say that they can be made worth that here!"

"Undoubtedly," answered Dickson. "I will take every hickory butt on your plantation over six inches in diameter, as soon as I can get under way here, at ten dollars per cord."

"Why there are a thousand cords on this plantation alone!" said Paul.

"I do not care if there are ten thousand!" answered Dickson with energy; "the more the better at that price."

"But it can be bought here at a much less price," said my husband.

"Perhaps for a short time that may be true," said Dickson, "but the price will soon range at about ten dollars on account of the labor of cutting and hauling. You see, only one or two 'cuts' from the butt of each tree can be used. The tree must be sawed down, because that heavy-grained swell at the very butt of the tree is by far more valuable than any other part. They are heavy, hard things to handle and draw, so that the whole matter of getting the timber out is one of hard work. If a man gets anything for his timber standing, he must have about ten dollars for it at the mill."

" And do you think there is a demand for all the handles, and the like, which could be made out of these forests of hickory?" asked Paul.

" Now," said Dickson, "let me tell you this is not a matter of a moment's thought with me. I have studied it, thoroughly and carefully. You see, when the war came on I was in a business that promised me a fortune, I thought. I had always worked hard and done well,—very well, I thought, for a man who had his own way to make,—and had got together some money a year or two before the war. I had a chance to put this into a business which I supposed would have left me independent before this time, and given me a chance to start my children without their having to work as hard as I had done. My wife had worked hard too ; not rough dragging work, it is true ; but she had engineered the household as few women can, and had made my dimes go further than many another man's dollars. She had always kept up good heart, too, and I never came

home tired and discouraged that I did not find
her bright and cheery, and I started out next morning stronger and more determined than I had
ever been before. So you may well imagine I was
anxious to make a fortune in order that she might
enjoy it."

The captain's dark face shone tenderly as he
spoke thus of his wife, and I will own that one of
his listeners forgot at that instant his nativity.

"Well," he continued, "the war came on and
our business happened to be one of those which
suffered. We held up as long as we could, but
finally, in the spring of '62, I sold out one day to
my partners for just enough to keep my wife and
children comfortable for a year and pay off a bal-
ance on the house and lot I had bought, and went
and enlisted.

"The next day I was off, and during the re-
mainder of the war I was all the time in some
part of the South. Of course I brooded on my
loss a good deal. My few thousands were not
much in themselves, but they were all I had, and
it was hard to think of having to go again through
all the struggle they had cost me. However, I
knew I must do it; and as I always expected the
war to end just as it did I had my eyes open to

see what chance there might be for a man to pick up a good thing down here. Being a wood-worker by trade, I naturally looked at the timber, among other things. I was struck with the pine that grows along the coast; but that requires a heavy capital and a good deal of time to turn out a heavy profit, and I have some doubts about it, then. There is a good thing in the black walnut and white pine of the mountain region when it becomes accessible—but that is away off yet; so I turned my attention to the hard woods of the lower slopes, where there are rivers and railroads to fetch and carry to and from the mill. I made up my mind when we marched through this Atlantic slope that there was many a fortune in these low-branching tough wide-grained oaks and hickories. I was not sure that the time for making them had quite come, however, because I did not know but there might still be a plenty of them nearer the established seats of trade and manufacture. Well, when the war was over I found that the few hundreds I had left my wife to live upon had increased in her hands until I had a snug little capital to begin life with again. I was full of this idea; but determined not to make another slip by not knowing all about my business, so I took up a sort of make-shift business, for the time, and set myself to find out all about hard woods and their uses. I have been about two years at it, and I think I know pretty much all there is to be learned on the subject. I am about as well versed in that as you are in the Indian-grave-yard business."

Paul winced a little, but still smiled and was flattered, as I saw, by the ready-witted reference of this practical man to his old hobby.

CHAPTER VIII.

THE WHITE WOODS.

" THE amount of hard woods or 'white woods' as they are called in trade, in contradistinction to the resinous woods and gums," said Dickson, " which are used in one form or another in the mechanic arts, in agriculture, and domestic life, is simply astounding to one who has never considered the matter. You have only to think how many handles of one sort and another—axe, pick, spade, plow, hatchet, hammer, etc.—are used on your own plantation, and apply that scale to the agricultural proprietors of the world, to see that one element of your incredulity is more fanciful than real. Then you have but to consider the vast number of mechanical pursuits in which these are indispensable. Think of the number of sledge and hammer handles that must be worn out in making cars, boilers, and engines, of the pick handles that must be had to build railroads, grade and pave streets, dig tunnels, sink shafts, mine iron and coal in Pennsylvania and England, gold in

California and Australia, and silver in Montana, and you will have some idea of the vastness of the uses of even handles alone. But this is only one of the various forms in which this product of nature is daily consumed by the insatiable demand of civilization. Cogs, pulleys and mallets, spokes and hubs, shuttles and bobbins, and a thousand specific devices for saving time or labor, must be made out of these woods. Take the single item of shuttles. There are not more than a half-dozen shuttle-makers in the United States, and, so far as I know, they manufacture only for our home use; and you are aware that but a small proportion even of our own cotton crop is spun and woven here. Yet I have just filled a contract for persimmon blocks to make into shuttles for one of these firms, which made nearly forty carloads.

"Think now of the innumerable vehicles all of which are to be supplied with spokes and hubs, rims and felloes, shafts, axles, spring-bars, coupling-poles, and other essential parts. You should remember, too, that there is no present likelihood of there being any substitute found for such woods in these uses. There will never be a metallic handle for axe or pick. The elasticity and lightness of wood are essential in all these uses. In others still other qualities, as a lack of friction or imperfect conduction, are necessary. Shuttles must be made of a closely-knit wood which may be worked very thin, yet remain firm and light and take a very high polish. Mallets, as for the use of stone-cutters, must be made of a heavy, close-grained, elastic wood, which will not splinter nor become indented from a long succession of hard blows upon the chisel head. There are but few kinds of wood which are adapted to any of these uses. Foremost among them all, as the great mechanical wood, is the hickory. Its whiteness, hardness, toughness, elasticity and durability, together with its capacity to assume a reasonable finish, and almost absolute freedom from splinters or checks, give it easily the supremacy over all other hard woods. It is true that in some of the uses to which these woods are devoted the hickory is not as good as some others. It would not make as good a shuttle as the persimmon, as good a plane-stock as the apple, as good a stamp or roller as the maple, as good an engraving material or as fine rings or croquet balls as the box or dogwood; but while these woods excel it in these peculiar uses, they are useless in a thousand others where the hickory is unapproachable. As a material for all classes of handles, light spokes, rims and shafts—in short, whenever both stiffness and lateral elasticity are required together, it is without a rival. It is among woods what steel is among metals. Two kinds of oak, the white and post, are sometimes used for the grosser purposes in which the qualities of hickory are required, as large spokes, felloes, etc., as well as many other purposes to which it is peculiarly adapted. The ash is the only other elastic handle wood, and its tendency to split between the grains, as well as its unreliability, its variableness in quality, make it undesirable except for a few purposes—as the spade, pitchfork, and the like—where lightness is a requisite. Where solidity only is required, the beach, maple, holly, apple, and a few other woods may be used. Among the best of these inelastic woods, however, is the persimmon and dogwood.

" Not only are there few woods adapted to such purposes. but soil and climate make remarkable differences in the qualities of even these varieties. When I spoke of hickories, the other day, you wanted me to go on the river-bottom to see those which grew there. I went because I thought it would gratify you, knowing very well that only an inferior quality of hickory would be found there. The heavy, close-grained, low, wide-branching hickory of the upland is the cream of this variety. The same is true of the oak. Your old field hedge-row white oak is the finest quality of oak in the world. Your upland hickory, grown upon a brownish-red soil with a dark, round rock abounding in it, is the finest specimen of this variety I have ever seen. At one time the hickory of the New England hills was celebrated for strength and elasticity; but this has almost disappeared. The hickory of Western New York, known as Genesee Valley hickory, was also, for a time, the leading wood of the trade; but this is gone too. Perhaps the best of all these was that grown along the banks of the great lakes, but that also has become extinct. Then the river and creek bottoms of the West were put under contribution to supply the demand for this wood; but it was, in the main, of poor quality. Meantime, as you know, the South was shut out from competition in this, as in a thousand other industries, by the fact of slavery. So it results that while New England, the Middle and Western States have been almost denuded of their stock of available hard woods, the Southern States have a bountiful supply, yet untouched, and of the best quality, on both sides of the Alleghanies, and extending from the banks of the Ohio and Big Sandy to the shoals of the Tennessee, and from the knobs of Kentucky to tide-water in the Carolinas.

"Europe never had any wood to compare with our hickory in its peculiar qualities, and is now without any supply of hard woods which need be taken into consideration. Her stock of spokes, handles, etc., must come from abroad. What the forests of South and Central America might supply in this line it is impossible to say. They are for the present beyond the range of commercial venture.

"You see, therefore, Mr. Dewar, that the main supply of hard woods for the world must come, probably for the next fifty years, from that portion of the United States lying south of the Ohio and Potomac rivers."

"It would seem so," said Paul thoughtfully.

"Oh! there is no doubt of it," said Dickson. "Such hickory as that," he added, throwing a pebble against an old gray-backed tree, which stood against the lawn, "would be worth forty

dollars a cord in New York or Connecticut to-
day."

"How many handles would that tree make?"
asked Paul curiously.

"I can tell you in a minute," said the captain,
as he sprang up, drew a rule from a cunning little
pocket in the leg of his trousers, went down to
the tree and measured its diameter. Then glanced
sharply up and down the trunk, went around it,
tapping the bark familiarly with his rule, seemingly making a mental calculation as he came
back to the porch. "About four dozen axe, if
there are no knots or checks in it, perhaps as
many more sledge, and twice as many hatchet or
hammer handles."

"And what would they be worth?" asked Paul.

"They would average about two dollars per
dozen at present prices, I think," said Dickson.

I saw that my husband was making calculations
now.

Then the process and cost of manufacture and
sale were discussed at length, and the plans of
the enterprising Yankee fully explained.

"And how much capital will this require, Mr.
Dickson, asked Paul.

"Almost any amount can be profitably employed," answered the other; "but I think such an establishment might venture to start on about ten thousand."

"And have you that amount?" Paul asked.

"I can put in about half that at this time, but have no doubt I shall be able to find some one who will be willing to put in the rest."

"No doubt," said my husband musingly—and then they went back to a further discussion of the details of the projected business.

Before it was concluded my husband had determined to become a partner with his guest, if he could secure the funds. Somehow I had a notion that it would not be an entire success, though I could not tell why, but I saw it pleased Paul, and I was anxious that he should turn his attention to something not quite so slavish as he made his plantation work. So I was almost glad that he thought well of this venture.

That night, after our guest had retired, I went into the cabinet where Paul sat at his desk with a sheet of paper all covered with calculations before him, and, putting my arm on his shoulder, I said:

"You think well of this man's idea, Paul?"

"I cannot see why it is not a sound one," he replied.

"And you would like to engage in it with him," I continued.

"If, upon examining the matter for myself, I found his statements and estimates correct, I would," he said—adding regretfully, "if I had the means."

"Could you not borrow the amount?" I suggested.

"Ah! Sue, it is not now as in the old times—any one who borrows money now must give good security and pay a high rate of interest.

"Could you afford to borrow for this purpose if you had the oportunity?" I asked.

"I think I could," he replied.

Then I hinted at what I had meant to say from the beginning. I know my voice had been trembling in all those questions, and the hand on his shoulder would not lie still, do what I might.

"There is the plantation, Paul; might not that?"—I stopped, for I could go no farther. There was something in my throat, and my heart beat so wildly that I could not utter another word. I had all a Southern woman's love for her home, and all the instincts of my class rose up in opposition to the idea of hazarding the old place on a speculative venture.

Paul had heard and comprehended both words and tears at length. He sprang up and caught me by the wrists, with a grasp which liked to have crushed them. Yet nothing ever pleased me more than to feel that fierce grasp. The tears rained down my face, but they were tears of joy, as he must have seen as he peered down into my eyes. I believe my cheeks must have burned like a bride's receiving her husband's first kiss, I was so rapturously happy in my sacrifice, for so I counted it.

"Oh, you would not, Cousin Sue—you could not," he said eagerly, "risk this old plantation in such a venture."

"I would do anything to please you, Paul," I said, trying to get my head on his breast. But he held me off and said:

"No, no, Cousin Sue, it is not because I wish to speculate nor even because I care for wealth myself, that I desire to do this, but because I seem to see a way to restore you to the comforts and position you have lost. I would give my heart's blood, darling, to see you have the means of gratifying every wish again, and it is because this enterprise seems to offer an opportunity for this that I was wishing to engage in it."

"Then certainly I ought to be allowed to contribute," I said, desperately wrenching my hands loose, and burying my head on his bosom, sobbed hysterically. His arms closed about me in a clasp which was a benison, and that night my head was pillowed on his breast once more.

I think that Yankee captain must have thought there had been some necromancy about Hickory Grove over night, for he could not keep his eyes off me at breakfast; and when Paul offered to engage in the business with him, if it promised well after examination, he was thoroughly astounded. Paul went North and came back quite satisfied, as I knew he would be; for I had no doubt the captain was in earnest and perfectly sincere, and I had no idea that Paul would see, in such a matter, anything that had escaped his observation.

CHAPTER IX.

WIZARDRY.

I T was very soon arranged. The plantation was mortgaged, the money borrowed, and Paul Dewar and Hiram Dickson became partners in the business of the manufacture and sale of handles, mallets, spokes, etc., from hickory and other hard woods.

Captain Dickson did not belie my first impression. Whatever faults he may have had, a want of energy and application was not among them. Before the ink was dry with which they signed the contract of partnership, he had broken ground for the building which he had already planned. Early and late he was on the ground, superintending everybody; planning this, directing that, and urging everything. He was fruitful in expedients and never at a loss for means to do anything he wished to accomplish.

In an incredibly short time as it seemed to me, and to every one who had been accustomed only to our deliberate way of doing things, the building was up, the machinery, partly bought and partly made under his direction, was in position, a great, well dug, engine set up, a huge chimney built, and the river hills for miles around resounded with the piercing whistle which called the hands to work. Mr. Dickson was fond of saying that time was money; and surely no one more fully comprehended that truism than he. Even before the building was completed, indeed before it was hardly begun, he had advertised through all the country for hickory and persimmon timber, and for several weeks the great white hickory logs had been going past the Grove, drawn by all sorts of teams and in all sorts of quantities. The well-to-do farmer with his three or four horses brought his cord, or the poor cropper—colored or white— with his mule or horse, or yoke of steers, or perhaps mule and ox yoked together, or even the ox alone in harness, brought one stick, or two, or more, as he might. It mattered not to Hiram Dickson in what quantities it came. His rule was always at hand and his keen eye scanned and graded each stick, noting its imperfections or excellences and estimating its value accordingly. So that when the last brick was laid on the top of the huge chimney, the great engine in its place.

and the lathes and saws in position, there was a great pile of hickory logs about the building, waiting for the hungry teeth which were within to tear and rend them.

At length the factory was in operation, and I experienced a childish delight in watching it as it transformed rough logs into piles of smooth white handles. I used to take my little boy and sit for hours watching the busy machinery until every portion of it became almost as familiar to me as to those who had it in charge. I think the fact that I loved to watch it gave Paul an additional interest in his new employment. At any rate he soon became much absorbed in its success and anxious to promote its activity. Somehow it did not hurt me to see him going about in that busy factory—though roughly dressed like the operatives—as it had to see him delving on the plantation. It was false to all the traditions of my class, I knew, but it did seem to me a higher style of labor than the other. Some of our old neighbors laughed at my enthusiasm over the factory, and I could but confess that I was perfectly fascinated with it. They thought it was the prospect of sudden wealth which charmed me, but I think that had little if anything to do with the joy

I experienced in visiting the factory. If I were a man I am sure I should engage in some business connected with machinery. I am surprised that no poet has ever successfully portrayed the poetry of mechanical action. I am confident that I never felt so inspirited and poetical as when watching the machinery. There was the row of great black boilers, six of them lying side by side, with the glowing fires beneath, fed with the creamy white hickory sawdust and shavings which were constantly falling from the saws and lathes in the room beyond the stone wall which shut in these seething monsters. In the engine-room beside them was the massive bed framed to support the huge wheel. The crank was grasped by the polished piston-arm, which rushed back and forth and turned the great wheel sixty times a minute with untiring regularity. I timed it so often that I could detect a variance of only three or four revolutions in a minute without consulting my watch. It did this as smoothly and quietly as my boy's patent top spins upon glass or marble. You could hear a whisper, standing beside it, though the force was so great that it jarred the ground we stood upon. Two hundred horse-power was in that long, low iron frame and that broad wheel, connected with the nest of boilers only by a four-inch supply pipe, and with that long whirring shaft in the factory only by the broad rubber band which hugged the surface of the wheel. Had I not seen the mass of stone and the great square timbers on which it rested, and the huge bolts which went down into the solid stone and cement I should have wondered by what power it was held in place. Yet it made far less noise and fuss than the little steam pump in the corner, which looked beside it like a jeweled plaything for a lady's boudoir.

But it was in the factory itself that this power began to really show itself, in a hundred feet of shafting, with drums and pulleys turning three hundred times a minute, while belts and counter-shafts made saws and lathe-heads and the grinding wheels turn perhaps as many thousand times in the same period of time.

There was the constant hum and rush of restless wheels, the crash of resistless teeth and the hasty murmur of men, who could not lag in their movements, being ever crowded by the angry relentless arm of that insensate horrible fate beyond the wall.

You could stand and watch the great shaggy

barked hickory, which appeared almost as heavy and as strong as the iron which its steel-gray sides seemed to claim kinship with, stripped and torn and ground and polished until it became a pile of deftly curved, delicately rounded and swelled, creamy white handles.

First you saw the great log hung upon center pivots above a circular saw, over which it was thrust back and forth until for every three inches of the circumference there was a cut of equal depth towards the heart. Then these pieces were split off and roughly trimmed and shaped with saws, then they were put into lathes where a fierce running little saw tore away all the wood that remained beyond the limits and requirements of the pattern which guided its action. When this was done it was trimmed upon another saw at each end; then ground upon swift-running sanded belts until all inequalities were worn away; then it was polished upon an emery-belt, and finally waxed and finished on another; and, having been thoroughly seasoned in the dry-room, went to the packing-room to be assorted and packed for the market, which extended all over the United States and to many points in Europe. And all about flew the white chips from the lathes, and the flocky sawdust gathered in piles everywhere. It was all so neat and clean and airy, and yet so strong and relentless in its ceaseless rush and so wonderful in its transforming power! It was as if the gnomes and fairies had banded together in the broad daylight to disport themselves with the white-hearts of our Carolina "shag-barks." It was indeed a beautiful application of force, the transformation of a dozen cords a day of this stubborn wood into those ivory-looking handles.

The money which Paul had borrowed not being required to be paid back at once, all of the profits of the business went to its extension; and there rose about our factory a right busy and populous village. The vast amount of timber consumed, and its character, being that which was before accounted entirely worthless except for firewood, as well as the high prices paid for it, rendered the enterprise a godsend to our impoverished people. What they received for this, outside of the labor of cutting and hauling, was just so much *money found*, they were accustomed to say.

There was constantly such a look of *business* about the factory that it was almost impossible to believe that it was not coining money for its owners. Yet Paul did not lose the careworn, anxious look which he had had so long.

When he first borrowed the money he had taken out a heavy insurance policy on his life, to guard against accidents, as he remarked. I had not de-sired this. It always seemed to me as if I could never more enjoy wealth which had come to me through the death of one I loved.

The years went on—one, two, three. The business had greatly increased—the anxiety finally had faded quite out of Paul's face. It was just at the beginning of the season for the fall trade, and they had on hand a stock which for quality and quantity had never before been approached. When this was sold, Paul would draw his dividend and pay off his debts.

That was his plan—on the morning of the 17th of September, eighteen hundred and seventy-three.

CHAPTER X.

THE DELUGE.

EVERY one knows what then befell. Thousands upon thousands of hearts still mourn the unseen terrible visitation which, like the blight of pestilence, swept over the land, blasting hopes, desolating homes, and crushing the strongest and proudest in its path. How many who were rich before were poor afterwards! How many who were proud before have dwelt in the valley of humiliation since! How many a life of prudent, careful toil was in an instant wrecked! how many a bright outlook as suddenly overcast! How many a gray head bowed to the tomb! how many a young brow took on the silver badge of age as the result of that day!

We speak of the " panic" or the " crash," and it is as a belt of darkness to our minds in the brightness of the past. To the student of political economies it marks a readjustment of values. To the business man it is the beginning of a long period of depression under which thousands of

the best and staunchest of their class failed. To
the judges and lawyers it marks one of those
periodic waves of bankruptcy which are always
followed by an undertow of crime and demoraliza-
tion. To one who studies the human heart—its
miseries and misfortunes—bankruptcy is only less
sad than the wreck which follows war. It tells of
a more terrible blight than any other—a blight
which settles upon the strongest and fairest, and
invades the brightest homes. Oh, many a heart
mourns to-day in a sad and hopeless bitterness
the wounds of that day, and many another life
has gone out in darkness by reason of it.

That day the "panic" came. From that hour,
to how many men in every business was it as it
was with Paul and Captain Dickson—a struggle
for life! The hope of profit went out with the
first hint of the great convulsion. Can I live it
through? was the only inquiry of merchant and
manufacturer.

It was peculiarly hard upon the business in
which Paul was engaged, since the autumn is the
harvest to which all in that line look forward,
just as the farmer does, all the rest of the year.
The labor and expense of the year had been
performed and incurred in the hope of what

these months might bring—and they brought nothing.

What was made remained unsold, and what had been sold remained unpaid for.

The works were closed, and a struggle went on night and day to avert disaster. Every straw which could give a moment's breathing space was caught at and held to with a wild, vague hope that it might bring relief. Paul went on to the North and tried to secure aid. He was but one of thousands, and all were hopeless. Where all are smitten no one cares for another's wound.

I had become so infatuated with the works that I did not realize our danger—in fact, my confidence in Paul and the business was so great that I was just sure they could not fail. While he was gone and the works were idle I cheered my loneliness with the thought that he would come back strengthened and reinforced for the conflict. I thought I should see it in his eyes and hear it in his step before he spoke. He stayed away a long time, and I waited hopefully, yet with a great fear, as the days grew more and more, and yet he did not come.

I had been so proud of the busy factory, had been so happy in watching its rise and operation, that I could not bear to think of its going into other hands. It had grown so into our lives that it seemed like wrenching away a part of them to let it go. In the trouble which came from the contemplation of this catastrophe I had quite forgotten that our home itself might also be lost. It did not once occur to my mind that the mortgage which had been given was yet unpaid, and that the loss of a part involved a loss of the whole.

CHAPTER XI.

AN OLIVE BRANCH.

IT was February when Paul came back, unsuc-
cessful—as I knew he had been when I heard
his footstep on the porch. There came with him
a stranger, one of those scientific men who had
learned of my husband's familiarity with the
Mound Builders, had read what he had written
years ago, and was anxious to see the collection
he had made.

Professor Ware was one of those Northern men
who have no parallel in other countries, as I am
told and can well believe. He was a full, robust
man, with a quiet, self-poised look. Though yet
young he had seen more of the earth's surface,
and of the dwellers thereon, both of the past and
present, than often falls to the lot of mortals, and
had improved his opportunity by observing what
he saw with unexampled accuracy. In the domain of a half-dozen sciences he was a recognized
authority, and spoke with the positiveness of actual knowledge. Geology, mineralogy, archæol-

ogy, and I forget how many other ologies Paul told me were as familiar to his quiet visitor as my boy's face was to me. He had made science pay, too. While he had an absorbing desire to *know*, he had never forgotten that in order to do so he must first live, and that the prime element of scientific success was a sufficiency of this world's funds to carry out his ideas and verify his conclusions. At the very outset therefore he had, under circumstances of the greatest difficulty, made a scientific collection which a rich Northern college had been glad to secure at a price which was a fortune to the collector. It had cost him labor and self-denial, which he thus transformed into money and position.

Then he discovered mines and valuable deposits of one kind and another in which he secured an interest, and was counted then among the rich men of the city where he dwelt.

My husband had a vast respect for this gifted stranger, and he made himself so agreeable to us all who were at Hickory Grove that, for a few days, we almost forgot our trouble in the pleasure of his society. You know that when anything fresh and rare comes into our isolated country life it is sweeter a thousand times than the same en-

tertainment would be in the bustle and excitement of the city. He and Paul had visited the
mounds which had been opened and many which
had not, measured the skeletons, calculated the
size of missing parts, exchanged theories, made
new guesses, and were as talkative and merry as
two boys in holiday-time. Finally, I think in
sheer desperation for an excuse to remain longer
together, they took to hunting. The weather
was that delightful midwinter Indian summer,
which we so often experience in the Carolinas; the
birds were unusually numerous that winter, and
Paul had always been fond of this sport. His dogs
and equipments were of the best, and he keenly
enjoyed a trial of skill in the field. The bags
which they made showed very clearly that he had
no unworthy contestant, and I think that before
they had ended their second day's shooting scientific theories were at a discount with both. If
they talked of anything but birds and dogs and
guns as they smoked their cigars that night after
supper I did not hear it, though I was an atten-
tive and delighted listener. Paul seemed so unconscious of trouble that I quite forgot our danger, and was happier than I had dared to be before
since that terrible day in September.

That was the thirteenth day of February. I should have remembered it by the fact that the professor remarked, when the proximity of the 14th was alluded to, that he must write his wife a valentine. Then, between us, Paul and I told the story of his life, and our minds went back to the old untroubled days. I sat by Paul on a low ottoman, and he kept on smoothing and patting my hair with a grave troubled look long after our guest had retired. Then he took a lamp, and after giving me a kiss, went off into the cabinet alone. I knew what this meant. He wished to think or write without interruption. It was an intimation that I should go to bed and he would come when he had finished his meditations.

The next day Paul and the Professor were to have their final trial of skill. They started early. It was a beautiful morning, and I went out and saw them beat several fields which they had reserved for this last day of sporting. They were very evenly matched, and scored almost bird for bird for hours. With the passionate love of sport which is characteristic of Southern people, I took the liveliest interest in the strife, following on till I was quite tired out; and then sitting down on a rock I watched them as they went away from me beating a weedy stubble field which was the haunt of some fine coveys yet unbroken. With a Southern woman's admiration of physical excellence, too, I could not help thinking that I had never seen two fairer specimens of manhood than my Paul and the professor—an opinion which I have as yet seen no reason to change. I was proud of them both—proud of my husband and proud of his friend—not, I think, because of their relations to myself, nor because they were my people, but because I thought the world could not furnish a likelier pair.

The sunshine gleamed on their barrels, the puffs of smoke shot out, I heard the quick explosion and saw the poor "Bob-White" drop limp and dead from his swift flight into the brown ragweed below. I caught now and then their voices in exultant queries, broken laughter, or the ringing "Mark five! mark three!" as the birds rose.

It seemed to me a proud sight as those two men, lately enemies, the one famed in science, and the other a knight who had won his spurs in battle and worn them with honor in many another, faring on together in happy harmony.

After a time they passed out of my sight and I went back to the house light enough of heart.

CHAPTER XII.

NOTA BENE.

HARDLY had I reached the Grove when I saw some one turn from the main road towards the house. I knew it to be Sheriff James, and all my fears returned as he tied his horse at the rack and came leisurely up the path to the house. He was shown into the sitting-room where I was, and after some ordinary talk inquired for Paul. I told him he had gone from home, and offered no information as to his whereabouts. I did not know why he should want my Paul, and was determined that he should not learn through me where he was. He seemed somewhat embarrassed for a moment, and then, with the air of one who faces an irksome task, he said:

"Mrs. Dewar, I have a duty to perform which is very unpleasant, because I know it must be disagreeable both to yourself and your husband. I am required to serve these notices," handing me two legal papers, "one copy for yourself and the other for Mr. Dewar. I sincerely trust they may occasion you no inconvenience. I assure you that no one more deeply sympathizes with your husband's losses than I. Good-evening, madam."

He had been gone some moments before I ventured to look at the hateful papers he had thrust into my hands. I was completely ignorant of all legal forms, and had a peculiar horror of whatever smacked of the court-house or of law. I knew that the papers had something to do with our loss. The sheriff's words had implied that much. What their specific purpose was I had no idea. I looked at one of them. It was endorsed:

"Copy of notice for Mrs. Susan M. Dewar."

I opened it and read:

"MRS. SUSAN M. DEWAR:

"Take notice that unless the sum of five thousand dollars with interest due by notes secured by mortgage, on a certain tract of land, known as Hickory Grove, be paid to me within twenty days, I shall at the expiration of said time proceed to sell said premises, at public outcry, to satisfy said debt in accordance with the terms and conditions of said mortgage.

"PHILIP HOLDFAST.

"*Feb.* 10*th*, 1874."

I do not know how I managed to get through with it, but I did. The light went out of my life then. For the first time I realized that *our* home, *my* home, the dear old Grove, was to be sold! That we were to be absolutely homeless in the world! Whether I fainted or became simply stupefied I shall never know. I dropped those horrible notices there in the middle of the sitting-room floor and fled to my own room, more dead than alive. I took no note of the hours as they passed away. I lay upon my bed and moaned in a dull, hopeless agony. Husband, child, everything and every one was forgotten except the constant and terrible thought that my home, my childhood's home, the dear old Moyer place where generations of our family had lived and died—the dear, dear old Grove—was to be mine no longer. I do not think I thought of Paul once in all those long, terrible hours—hardly more than once of my child. The specter of poverty was before me, and death would have been a thousandfold more

welcome. It even occurred to me more than
once that the bright river which flowed past a
hundred yards away offered the easiest and surest
remedy for my ills. I did not put away the
thought. It was just pushed from my mind by
my present misery.

I saw, heard, thought of nothing beyond my
own room and my own heart until I heard the
report of firearms in the room adjoining my own
—my husband's cabinet! Then everything rushed
upon me with the vividness of light! I knew the
day had passed, Paul had come back, and read
the notices, and—crying, "Paul! Paul!" forgetting
everything else in the one thought that *he* had
felt the blow—I ran to the door of the cabinet,
burst it open only to see him prone upon the
floor with a pistol in his hand and the room full of
powder-smoke!

CHAPTER XIII.

"AS CHRIST LOVED US."

THE first one to enter the cabinet by the door opening from the porch was the Professor. I do not know whether he came in response to my scream—for I know I must have screamed—or because he had heard the explosion. I only know that he came and had no sooner entered the door and glanced at my face and then at the form on the floor than he seemed to comprehend every thing and, in his quiet way, decided what was best to be done. He closed and locked the door behind him, came quickly towards me, and said, meaningly:

"Send for a physician. Be quiet and admit no one."

His firm, quick tones reassured me and I let him go alone to my prostrate husband, while I went to the door of my bedroom where my maid, Parthenia, was already clamoring for admission, and, with a quietness which amazes me now, gave her the message he had charged me to deliver.

"But there is no one on the place, Miss Sue! The boys have all gone to meeting," said the girl.

"There is no time to go for a neighbor," I replied. "Get on Bob and go yourself." She was a young active girl, and a two miles' ride on the easy-going, sagacious thoroughbred was nothing to her.

"But you, Miss Sue?" she asked hesitatingly.

"I don't want anybody else to go. I shall get along till you return," I said.

"All right, then," she replied, flattered by the preference my words expressed, and she was off in an instant.

"Then I closed the door and rushed back to gaze on what I felt would blast my life and sear my eyeballs, yet which I must see, and oh! I shall never forget that terrible sight which greeted my eyes as I entered the cabinet again! Paul was lying in front of his desk, his face and the upper part of his body in the circle of light which the student's lamp attached to his desk cast on the floor. The eyes were turned upward and the great white face was set in rigid lines of agony. He had fallen on his side, but the Professor had turned him on his back and was examining his head and chest.

Even death could not rob the countenance of my Paul of its noble tenderness, or the woe which had overwhelmed even his strength.

For once I forgot myself, and a wild tide of remorse swept across my breast as I gazed on that cold, fixed face with its stony, unseeing stare, and thought that it was my selfish grief which had left him to meet the terrible shock alone. I felt that he had sacrificed himself for love of me—because he could not endure to witness my distress at our misfortune.

Oh! it was terrible to think that I had let so noble a heart burst from very dread of witnessing my needless sorrow! How had I mistaken my noble Paul! Oh! I forgot myself only to wish that I were lying there beside him—his bride in death—now, for the first time, comprehending his love and tenderness. I even looked for the pistol I had seen in his hand with a vague idea that I would go to him still,—that he must be lonely in the great uncertainty to which he had gone. I was so eager to let him know how, more than ever, I loved him, to tell him that I never had a thought of blaming him for our misfortune, which, as you know, was quite untrue, yet what woman ever winced at falsehood when it would comfort

the heart she loved? And then, too, it was not
I who had blamed him, but the selfish, foolish
something which had possessed my mind in those
first moments when the bitter knowledge of our
loss came to my consciousness.

The pistol was not there. I ran forward and
fell on my knees on the other side of Paul. The
Professor was on his knees with Paul's head in his
lap. All this I saw and thought and did in a
flash. I do not suppose I paused an instant after
shutting the bedroom door. I clasped my arms
about his neck, half shuddering lest I should feel
his blood upon them, and fell upon his dear, dead
face with clinging kisses, muttering Paul! Paul!
Paul! with a wild, fierce thought that his spirit
would hear my impassioned, yearning cry and
come back from the bourne it had just passed.

I felt that he was dead. I had no doubt of that.
Yet I thought that he could hear me, that he
would know my thought and come back when he
saw how much greater was my agony at his departure than at the misfortune we had suffered.
So I clung to him and cried protestingly:

"I did not blame you, Paul! It is nothing,
Paul! Why did you leave me? Come back to
your cousin Sue—oh! Paul! Paul!"

Suddenly I felt the Professor's hand upon my arm. How terribly strong he was! Even in my excitement I felt each finger as it cut into the flesh. A week after I saw the bloody imprint and blest the hand that made it.

"Let go!" he cried hoarsely, as he tore my clasped hands apart and thrust me back from the face of my dead. "Be still. You do not know what you are doing!"

I looked up in an amazement which overcame every other feeling. His face was ashy pale, his lips close shut, and his eyes burned with a strange, fierce light which hushed me in an instant. I have thought since that the prophet's face must have shone like that when he took the widow's son "from her bosom and carried it into a loft where he abode." I could not help but do as he wished. I obeyed him as I would have obeyed my Paul if he had spoken at that moment. I relinquished my clasp of the dear head and looked up into the stern face above, appealingly, it must have been—for something of pity came into the Professor's eyes, and, I thought, something of hope too, as he gathered Paul in his arms and raised him from the floor. He was so strong that the nerveless form did not seem to burden him.

"Bring a lamp," he said sharply, with an imperious glance at me. I obeyed silently, and he
carried Paul and laid him on my bed. I could
but moan as I saw him arrange his head upon the
pillow. "Hush! Hold the light," he said hurriedly. He ran a hand over Paul's head once
more.

Then he pulled off his collar, tore open his shirt
front, and thrust a hand in upon his breast,—took
it out and gazed at me a moment half doubtfully.

"How far is it to the physician's?" he asked.

"Two miles," I answered.

"Too far, too far," he muttered.

Too far! I caught the words, and a strange
wild hope took hold of me for an instant, but
faded as quickly when I glanced at the rigid face
upon the pillows.

The Professor walked across the room once or
twice absently, then came close to me, took the
lamp from my hand and set it on the bureau at
the foot of the bed. Then he put both hands on
my shoulders, and looking into my eyes steadily
said in a voice which trembled with earnestness,

"How strong are you?"

"Ah! oh!—I am very weak," I answered gasp-
ingly.

"But if there was no one else," he said, "if there was no one else who *could* do it, what would *you* do to save his life?"

"To save his life! oh—you—you do not"—I think I should have fainted if he had not shaken me.

"Hush!" he said impetuously, "I do not say it can be done, but if it could—if there was a chance, what would you do? What would you undertake?"

For the first time, then, I felt that he was all a-quiver with excitement. I understood then, and all at once I felt that my intuition had been correct, that I should call back my Paul. I was quiet enough now. My nerves were as calm as they are at this instant. I looked steadily in his eye and answered,

"Everything."

"Ah!" he said with a sigh of relief, "that is right. I am glad to hear you speak thus. And now, Mrs. Dewar, will you trust your husband's life in my hands? When the physician comes it may be too late."

"It could not be in truer ones," I answered without hesitation.

"Thanks," he said in his quick jerky way.

"You must help me. Do not flinch or waver, whatever happens. Hold the light."

I took the lamp and held it towards him. He took out a knife and examined the blades by its light. I did not think of trembling or doubting. I was sure he would save Paul. He seemed satisfied with his examination. I think he made it more to test me than the blades.

"All right," he said. "Hold the light here."

He turned to the bed and tore the clothing from my husband's right arm. I hardly comprehended his purpose till he had grasped it close with his left hand and strained the skin between palm and finger and made a swift incision with his knife. I knew then his purpose was to bleed him. Only a few sluggish drops crept out from the severed vein. The Professor sat watching it intently and with a look of disappointment.

"That will not do," he muttered, "something else must be done. Quick, Mrs. Dewar!" he cried, "bring me two of those tall glasses I saw on your side-board yesterday."

I flew into the dining-room and brought back two of the long, slender ale glasses of a former generation. Then he turned Paul's head upon one side and made a dozen or so shallow cuts upon his temple, swiftly and deftly. Then he caught the lamp from me, ran into the cabinet, and came back with a half-dozen sheets of tissue paper in his hand. Giving me the lamp again, he loosely twisted one of them into a ball, lighted it at the chimney of the lamp and thrust it into one of the glasses which he clapped bottom upwards on Paul's temple. The paper blazed a moment, then shriveled into a white ash, and we saw the dark blood flowing out and quenching its last spark. The Professor gave a sigh of relief.

"We shall save him, I think," he said, in firm, even tones.

I did not answer—I could not.

The operation was repeated again and again on both temples and both sides of the neck. At length Paul sighed, then breathed irregularly. The blood had trickled down upon his face, and added to its ghastliness, but when a fluttering motion came into the eyelids, and the fixed orbs moved uncertainly and aimlessly, it was as glorious a sight to me as the face of the Master shining like the sun to the wondering watchers on the Mount of Transfiguration. I knew that Paul would live. It is not necessary to tell what happened next. If it were, I could not, except from hearsay,

Sometime afterwards I found myself lying on the sofa feeling " powerful weak," as our country people say, with my hair dripping, my face feeling as if it had been rubbed with spirit, and a handkerchief, drenched with cologne, tucked under my nose, while Parthenia was fanning me anxiously.

On the other side of the room two men were standing by the bed, the family doctor on the side with his back towards me, and the Professor with his arms crossed upon the foot-board, looking contented and nonchalant.

CHAPTER XIV.

SCIENCE AND ART.

MY husband was lying in the bed now, his head curiously wrapped up, as I could see, and the old doctor evidently just examining his condition and hearing a report of his treatment.

"Repeated cuppings, cold applications to the head and warm ones to the extremities—really, sir, the profession could have done no more for him than you have. I do not see that anything more is to be done at present," said the doctor.

"But the bullet," I said, weakly and wonderingly, "what about the bullet?"

"What, eh?" said the old doctor, peering at me over his spectacles.

"She has persisted all the time that she heard a shot when her husband fell. She told me so when I first came into the room on hearing her scream," said the Professor, with a quiet and apparently sympathetic mendacity. "I suppose she was asleep in here, and hearing the fall perhaps dreamed of the shot. You know, Doctor, the sleeping mind not unfrequently plays such pranks."

"Certainly—certainly. There is no bullet in this case," said the doctor. "Your husband was not born to be hurt by bullet, Mrs. Dewar."

"No bullet?" I said dreamily.

"No indeed," he responded; "only a sudden congestion, something like a slight apoplexy."

"No bullet! apoplexy!" I could not understand it. Had I been dreaming, or had I really heard that shot and seen that pistol?

"I am afraid," said the Professor, crossing to the sofa and laying his hand upon my head, "that this sudden shock has prostrated you almost as much as it has your husband. I think you should dismiss all thought from your mind and try and restore yourself by rest, so as to aid him, when he shall recover consciousness, by your presence and demeanor."

The doctor also came over and felt my pulse and laid his hand on my head caressingly.

"Yes, yes, poor dear, you may sleep now," he said. "It's been a terrible strain I know, but you and Mr. Ware have saved Paul's life. No doubt of that. And now, as he says, you must go to sleep so as to be fresh for the cheerful nursing he will require hereafter. Leave him to us now. We will take care of him."

The kind old doctor, with all his shrewd guessing, was a victim of the Professor's guile. I saw this and was almost afraid he was cheating me. I was sure his purpose was kindly, but could not quite fathom it.

A sleeping draught was prepared for me, and with the Professor's help and that of my girl Parthenia, I was removed to my mother's old room.

It was a dreamless sleep which I had that night, and the day was several hours old when I awoke next morning, cheerful and refreshed. It was some time before I could remember what had occurred. When I did I sprang up and hastily throwing a wrapper about me, ran to the door of my room. As I opened it the Professor came forward with quick noiseless footsteps and laid his hand upon my arm. The room was silent and dark.

"Paul? Paul?" I whispered fearfully.

"He is doing well and sleeping now," answered the Professor, still barring my entrance.

"Can I not see him?" I entreated.

"The doctor has only just retired, Mrs. Dewar,"

he answered firmly, "and left me the most posi-
tive instructions that I must permit no one to
enter the room, especially you. He says it is of
the last importance that he should be undisturbed.

"But I will not disturb him," I pleaded, "just
one look."

But the watcher was firm. Of course I had
recourse to woman's last argument, tears. But
he would not yield. Then I became indignant,
and asked him if I had not shown enough of self-
control the night before to be trusted this much
now.

"Will you exercise the same control now?" he
asked.

I promised eagerly.

"And you will not speak to him, nor touch
him?"

Again I promised. He stepped aside and I
passed into the room and around to the bedside
of my dead who was alive again.

The Professor went to the window and opened
a tiny crevice in the curtain, so I could see the
face of my beloved, dimly, but I could see that he
was alive still. I remembered my promise, but
with difficulty restrained myself from kissing
the poor relaxed lips or calling upon the dear

name. He seemed to feel my presence, however, for presently his lips moved and he said
feebly,

"Sue! Cousin Sue!" and he reached down
upon the bed-clothing with his right hand which
was next me, as if feeling for me. That was too
much. I fell on my knees and took his dear hand
in mine and pressed it softly to my lips. The
Professor came towards me with a whispered word
of caution. I did not say a word or move again,
only held the poor nerveless hand to my cheek
while the tears rained over it and a torrent of
wild prayers and ecstatic thanks welled silently
up from my heart.

"Sue! O Sue! did you get it?" asked Paul
weakly and anxiously.

I felt the Professor's hand on my shoulder and
was motionless and silent. The poor head turned
anxiously from side to side, and again the weak
voice quavered brokenly out, "Did—you—get—
it, Sue? Did you get the—the—the—insurance,
darling?"

The Professor's grasp tightened on my shoulder
and he whispered excitedly in my ear:

"Tell him yes, for God's sake, and speak naturally, cheerfully."

I comprehended his purpose, but God only knows how I got strength to comply.

"Oh yes, darling," I said, "that is all right. I got it, Paul! I got it!"

"Thank—God," he whispered, with a sigh of relief. His features relaxed and his breathing became that of contented slumber.

The Professor took Paul's hand from my embrace and led me from the room. As he closed the door behind me I asked fearfully,

"Have I done him any harm?"

"On the contrary, I hope much good," he replied, "Keep up your heart," he added cheerfully, "and when the doctor comes to relieve me let me have a few minutes' conversation with you in the cabinet. You know I was to have left to-day," he said in answer to my look of inquiry.

"But you will not?" I said anxiously.

"We will talk of that," he said smilingly, "when you have breakfasted and I am released from duty here."

CHAPTER XV.

THE KEYSTONE.

SOMEHOW I could not help feeling cheerful. Paul was sick, very sick I knew, but he was alive and I had thought him dead. He had come back to me as from the grave. So I ate my breakfast in thankfulness; but I could not help thinking of all that had happened since Paul, the Professor and I sat there at breakfast the day before. Then I wondered if it could be that I had dreamed about that shot and the pistol I had seen in his hand. It could not be. I had recognized the pistol. It was one of those queer repeating Derringers, with one barrel above the other, which a friend had presented to Paul just after the war. I had often seen it, and had sometimes fired it just to please Paul, who had an idea that every woman and child should be taught to shoot and swim, as one can never tell when one may need such knowledge to save life. I knew where it was kept in his desk, as he had often shown me in order that I might know where to find it should I ever need it in his absence. I would soon determine this matter. I would go and see if it were there now.

I hastened to the cabinet. The drawer of the desk in which the pistol had been kept was open. It was not there. I was right. I had not been dreaming. I sat down in the arm-chair before the desk to think. As I did so my eyes fell upon a paper lying on the desk. I knew it at a glance. It was one of the notices the sheriff had given me the day before. My premonitions had been correct, then. He had found this paper where I had dropped it, and his shame and agony had goaded him to the terrible deed. Yet they told me he was not shot. They surely were mistaken. How could I have been so thoughtless as to have dropped that paper! I might have known that this blow would drive him to desperation. I reached forward and took the paper intending to tear it into fragments. As I did so an envelope lying beneath it attracted my attention. It was directed in Paul's handwriting:

> *Sue M. Dewar,*
> *Per St. Valentine.*

I opened it and read:

A WIFE'S VALENTINE.

The days have passed in ceaseless flow,
　Morning and evening, sun and shade,
Till the years have grown to the long ago,
　Since, awkward lover and artless maid,
At the game of hearts together we played,
　Defiant of Time and Woe.

The boy—I grieve to think—is dead,
　Urned in dust of the holy past—
And only a man is left instead,
　Busy and burdened and overcast
With clouds of care, as dark and vast
　As the winter midnight overhead.

I sometimes hope he is still within,
　Closely screened from the careless gaze,
Hiding away from the ceaseless din,
　The turmoil of manhood's weary ways,
The clangor of strife and the coil of sin ;
　But much I misdoubt if he really stays.

The boy besought thy love to bless
　The fancied woes of Valentine !
The *man* unto his heart would press
　With rapture, as a thing divine,
Sorrow or crime or nothingness,
　To give one moment's joy to thine !

Would dwell eternally with Shame,
　And count its rankest savor sweet ;

Would bare his heart-strings unto flame,
    And Want and Death would gladly meet,
To give thee joy—or yield thee fame !
    Nor ask to kiss thy dimpled feet !

Yet, ah ! the lines of carking care
    Are creeping, creeping round thine eyes
And in the meshes of thy hair—
    Nay, start not, nor pretend surprise—
Which was so bonnie brown and fair,
    The glint of envious silver lies !

Oh ! dead boy-love, whose warmth could bring
    To loving lips and heart forever
The roundelay of birds in spring,
    Pulsing with sinless passion's quaver,
And o'er the worshiped features fling
    A glamour fading never !

Oh ! woe that manhood's strength but brings
    Embittered sweetness to Love's shrine !
God grant that memory sometimes sings—
    Though cumb'ring cares our lives entwine,
And Sorrow sweeps the minor strings—
    Of him—thy boy-love—Valentine !

It was signed " Paul."

CHAPTER XVI.

THIS INDENTURE WITNESSETH.

MY poor darling had come the night before, while I slept, and written those lines, intending to send me another valentine. And he thought I did not love him so well as I had in the old days. As if that could be compared to the later love! He thought because the world and care had come into my life—perhaps because I had reproached him, and had not sought him when he withdrew himself from me—that my love was less. Oh! I could see how I had let the great fond nature squander and torture itself, unmindful of the treasures which that sensitive, too sensitive soul poured at my feet. I had misunderstood him. Knight as he was in conflict, a Bayard in arms, he was of too fine a fiber to love the harsh contact with the world. He could do or suffer with the utmost zeal and cheerfulness, but the rough, sordid struggle with the world sickened him. He could give his life for a principle that he cherished or for a friend that he loved as gladly as a bride-groom goeth to his nuptials.

He had thought I blamed him for our misfortunes, and his sensitive spirit had shrunk away from me and he had devoted his life to reinstating me in wealth and position. He thought that as I had been reared in luxury I prized it more than I did his love. I ran through our whole life as I sat there by the desk, at which he had spent so many hours and performed labors of which I was yet to learn, and saw how I had neglected and misappreciated the noble being who counted himself but dross in comparison with my poor, weak, selfish self. Yet I had not meant to be selfish. I *did* love him better than of old, only he had kept his heart so hidden that I had only now and then caught a glimpse of it. We had lived apart, though together; coolly, though both our hearts were full of love. We had each repressed our impulses from a misconception of the other's feelings. Day by day we had swung apart, while we both daily yearned for a closer communion. We had both been but a bundle of contrarieties, and it was all my fault too. I knew, or ought to have known, what an innocent, simple, blundering soul my giantly Greatheart was!

Would he ever have found out my love if I had

not done the wooing? Did he not live year after year with the incense of my adoration going up about his nostrils, and never dream that he was the deity to whom it was offered? Did I not remember what a great unconscious, self-forgetful, self-depreciating oaf he was years before? Did I not know that the laurels he had won in the long war-struggle were all forgotten, that he counted himself less a hero than thousands of those who had followed his lead and drawn inspiration from his devotion? But now—well, never mind; if my Paul but lived he should know how much more I loved him than wealth, luxury, children, friends, or all of life besides.

I wiped my eyes as I made these good resolutions, which came so late, and read again through another mist of tears my husband's valentine.

As I laid it down another envelope upon the desk attracted my attention. It was a large white official-looking one, endorsed in many styles of ornamental letters, the blanks filled up with exquisite penmanship and underscored with red lines—a marvel of typographical and calligraphical art. One glance at it froze my bounding blood with horror! It was all plain to me then—

the great loving, self-forgetful heart—the agony, the pistol! O God!

The words, the lines—the very stains and folds of that envelope—were seared into my brain in that terrible instant, never to be effaced. I can see it now, every terrible letter and figure which it bore is clear to my memory.

It was endorsed:

> *Policy on the life of*
> *Paul Dewar.*
> *Amount* $40,000.

My Paul, my husband, my hero, had intended to destroy his life that I might be enriched by his death!

CHAPTER XVII.

MOUND-BUILDERS TO THE RESCUE!

THE Professor came in while I sat there petrified with horror. A few words explained to him, as far as was necessary, the facts I had learned.

"Alas," he said when I had concluded, "it is as I feared. I hoped I might keep a knowledge of it from you and so put the pistol in my pocket, intending if I had found that he had really inflicted a wound upon himself to have invented some means to keep it from your sight, for a time at least. He had probably taken the pistol in his hand for the purpose of self-destruction when his nervous excitement culminated in something resembling apoplexy and in his fall it was discharged, fortunately without harm to himself."

"You are not deceiving me then?" I said. "He is really not wounded at all?"

"He has no wounds except those which were made with your consent and assistance," he answered smilingly.

"And for which I must thank—"

"God," he interjected solemnly; and I bowed a tearful assent, though I doubt not my eyes spoke my gratitude to the human agent. Then he began to search among the cases and shelves.

"If we can find," he said, "the course of the bullet, we may form some idea of the position he was in when the shot was fired. He may simply have had it in his hand when he fell, without the intention we have attributed, and it may have exploded on striking the floor or some other obstacle."

I watched him absently as he pried about among the many relics contained in the cabinet of primeval means of destruction, for the traces of the modern life-destroyer, that terrible Derringer ball, which had found a resting-place somewhere among them.

"Ah! here is a trace of it," he said as he showed me where it had crushed through the skull of a Mound-Builder, "I can almost fancy the surprise of the old Pre-Adamite," he added jocosely.

Then he went on following the clue thus obtained, and I fell into a dull, sad reverie. I could not shut out from my mind that our situation was indeed deplorable. That which had driven Paul to desperation I could not ignore.

I was startled by the voice of the Professor at my elbow.

"This is a very valuable collection which your husband has made, Mrs. Dewar."

I looked up with a sudden hope and asked eagerly:

"Do you think so!"

"Undoubtedly. It needs some skill in preparation and arrangement, but the elements of a valuable collection are here. Do you think he could be persuaded to part with it?"

Persuaded to part with it! The idea that one who would offer his life for the comfort of those he loved should need persuasion to induce him to sell a lot of old musty relics! I knew the specimens had many of them cost Paul a great deal of time and money. He had frequently told me that some of them were unique, that there were none others like them in the world; but I had never thought that they might prove an assistance to us in our present strait. I am sure my voice must have trembled as I asked, not daring to look up:

"What do you think they would be worth?"

I waited with a beating heart for a reply, hardly daring to hope that he would name any considerable sum.

"Well," he said deliberately, "from the examination I have given it, I think I should be willing to give ten thousand dollars."

"Ten thousand dollars!" I exclaimed. Had the days of miracles returned? Was I dreaming? I could scarcely believe myself awake, but the voice of the Professor recalled me.

"I have no doubt," he said, "that it cost your husband much more; a man who makes a collection just *con amore*, without a careful study of his expenditure, never knows its cost, and is almost certain to subject himself to great losses."

I looked up at him and saw that his eyes were fixed on me with a peculiar earnest look. As mine fell again they rested for a moment on the Sheriff's notice on the desk. All at once it flashed into my mind that this rich man was making our old cabinet, which Paul and I had been so happy in collecting, an excuse for offering us charity. I thought he had become so interested in my husband that he would *give* him all these thousands, and take the cabinet as a pretended consideration. All my foolish Southern pride rose in an instant. I stood up and looked at him, I doubt not, angrily, though I was grieved—for I loved this man and appreciated his motive. Paul loved him too, and he had just saved Paul's life for me. So I think tears got the better of pride when I spoke.

"You should not take advantage of our misfortune to humiliate us."

"Indeed," he said, with troubled earnestness, "indeed I had no thought of doing so."

"Did you not know our circumstances? Have you not read that?" I said, excitedly thrusting the notice towards him.

He glanced over it and said:

"I had not seen this. I did know your husband was in straitened circumstances, and—and—"

"And you would never have made this offer but for that fact!" I said tremblingly, hoping that he would deny it.

"I confess I should not," he answered frankly.

"Enough, Professor," I said, as proudly as I could. The man had been so kind and true he had almost earned the right to put his hand in his purse to help our need, and I would not have pained him for the world. I believe that had I consulted my own heart I should have accepted his bounty; but I remembered the proud sensitive one which beat unconscious of my temptation in the room beyond, and thought that it would break indeed should I so condescend, for I knew my pride was but as a drop in the ocean when compared to his. "Enough, Professor Ware; we have not yet fallen so low that we can accept charity, even from you. We must face our misfortune and do our best." I attempted to pass him and leave the room.

"Stop," he said, laying his hand on my arm, "There is surely some mistake. Charity? What do you mean?"

"What do I mean?" I asked. "Why, Professor, you have just acknowledged that you would not have made this offer but for our being in reduced circumstances; in other words, that you made the cabinet an excuse for offering us pecuniary aid."

"Ah, yes; I see," he said, with a sort of relieved chuckle and a queer twinkle in his eyes. "Please be seated, Mrs. Dewar, and let us talk farther."

"I hope, Professor Ware—" I began.

"I think I have the right to ask that much," he said with dignity, almost sternness.

I obeyed at once. Had he not saved my Paul?

Besides, a woman likes to obey a man who
"speaks as one having authority." I imagine that
was the reason so many women believed on the
Saviour at the first. He sat down too, and after
a moment said in a cold, even tone, without looking at me:

"Mrs. Dewar, the reason I said that I would
not have made such an offer for the cabinet if I
had not been aware of your unfortunate circumstances was because I understood something of
that same foolish pride which you have just ex-
hibited."

"Professor Ware!" I said excitedly.

"Do not force me to claim what is my due,"
he said significantly. I twisted my fingers and
waited. I was certainly in bonds to him, and
would not disown them.

"I am going to tell you now what I should
have told your husband but for the sad event of
last night. This cabinet is considered the best
collection of Indian curiosities and archæological
specimens referring to the past of our own land
that there is in the world. Your husband was an
indefatigable collector, and a man of wonderful
fertility and research in his own field, but he lacks
the mechanical skill and knowledge requisite to

make such a collection command its full value. When this is done the museum of antiquities will be worth from $15,000 to $20,000. In their present condition the geological specimens are of little value—few of them are named, and not all that are, are correctly done. Many of them are, however, splendid specimens—and all of them, I believe, are labeled with the place and date of finding. The whole needs to be catalogued."

"There is a catalogue," I said, "referring to every specimen by number. I made it myself," with some pride.

"Indeed!" with a smile.

"I mean under Paul's direction," I said.

"Of course," he resumed; "then that would add somewhat to its value. The geological specimens I can put into an incomplete collection I am under engagement to furnish, and make valuable in that manner. Now, Mrs. Dewar, I knew of your husband's circumstances and came on here expressly to buy this collection. I should not have offered to buy it if he had not been in those circumstances, because I should have expected to find him too proud to sell. Instead of being *charity*, it is with me a pure matter of business."

"Oh! Professor, I beg your pardon," I cried,

seizing his hand and laughing and crying at once.
I am not sure but I kissed it, for my mind was in
a perfect hubbub—indeed I *might* have done so, if
it had not been.

"Do not misunderstand me, Mrs. Dewar," he
said, with that provoking twinkle in his eyes.
"While the amount to be paid is merely a matter
of business with me, yet I must confess that since
I have become acquainted with your husband I
have come to regard him so highly that I have
been very anxious that he should accept my proposition and relieve himself from embarrassment
thereby. You see I am bound to make it a matter of charity as well as business."

"Oh! spare me!" I cried, still holding his
hand and weeping for joy. "I am sure I can
never thank you enough for not being angry at
my folly."

CHAPTER XVIII.

"WHERE IS THE WAY WHERE LIGHT COMETH?"

WELL, the end of it all was that I sold the Professor the cabinet at his own price; he saying that he knew Paul would be glad to ratify anything that I did, and giving me his check at once for the amount, though he refused to remove any portion of it until Paul had recovered sufficiently to be told of it lest it should annoy him that we had disturbed it during his illness.

A few days afterwards I asked the Professor how he came to know about my husband's pecuniary embarrassment.

"Well," he said, " I do not know that I ought to tell you, but as I think it was a good act and kindly meant, I believe I will risk it. The fact is, a gentleman who had seen this cabinet but who had no accurate idea of its value came and spoke to me about it last fall. Of course as soon as he mentioned it I knew all about it, as much as one could know about a collection he has never seen and of which no catalogue is published. You know I have made the collection of museums a business. Well, he said that your husband had gone into some manufacturing business which he was afraid would prove a loss to him, and he thought he might save himself from losing his plantation, which was mortgaged for part of the capital invested, by making sale of the collection. He wanted me to get acquainted with your husband, and as delicately and carefully as I could hint to him this method of extricating himself from his difficulties, if the collection was of sufficient value. When your husband came North, therefore, this gentleman wrote me where he was staying and gave me a letter of introduction to parties who made us acquainted, since he did not wish to be known in the matter."

" How did it come to take you so long to make up your mind?" I asked.

" Well, of course I wanted to look the collection over. It required some time to do this, naturally ; and when I had done so and made up my mind and began to hint at the value of the collection I found it quite impossible to get your husband to take my intimations as they were intended."

I could but laugh at this and tell him of our courtship.

"Yes," said the Professor, as I concluded, " I found his to be one of those great simple natures which are so true and brave that a hint is lost on them. They are so direct themselves that they cannot understand indirectness in others. I had come to think so highly of him that, aside from the purchase I desired to make and the solicitations of the gentleman who had planned the whole thing, I was very anxious not to fail in the undertaking. Yet I was afraid to come straight out, as I ought not to have been perhaps, and make the proposition to him directly, but put it off from day to day with the idea that I might ingratiate myself more completely into his confidence and have a better prospect of ultimate success. I had decided to broach the matter to him that very night, when I was to have a conversation with him in regard to the publication of his book."

"His book!" I cried, in amazement.

"Certainly," said the Professor, " did you not know he had a volume nearly ready for the press?"

"No, indeed," I answered.

"He must be a strange man, if he can keep such secrets from you," he replied smilingly ; " but as we have taken some liberties with his peculiar domain since his illness, and as I happen to know where he keeps the manuscript, I will treat you to a farther surprise if you desire."

He picked up my husband's keys which lay upon the desk as he spoke, and, as I did not object, opened one of the drawers and showed me a great pile of manuscript, written on one side in my husband's honest, unpretentious hand, yet plain as print. There were many hundred of these pages.

"It is a great work," said the Professor, "and executed with wonderful care and faithfulness. It will put his name in the very front rank of scientific writers whenever it is published. Its financial success cannot be foretold. The cost of publication will be great and his direct profits may be inconsiderable. It will open the doors of the future to him, however, and assure the success of what he may do hereafter. I only wonder when he found time to do it."

Alas! I did not. The secret of his isolation and preoccupation was disclosed to me then. I knew why he had left me night after night to shut himself into the cabinet. I knew why his lamp had shone far past the noon of night and his

hushed tread came to my ears so often in the
early dawn. Oh! how humbled and unworthy I
felt that I had let him labor thus alone and in silence, without aid or sympathy; that a stranger's
eye had first seen his work and a stranger's ear
first listened to his aspirations. Why had not my
love so clung about his heart that it had known
the birth of his hope and the dawning of his ambition? Ah, me! Had I been his wife, or only
a stranger within his gates?

I had one more question to ask the Professor,
as to who was this friend of Paul's who devised
this little scheme for our benefit.

"Ah! that is just what I was desired not to
tell," he said, "and I am not sure I did not promise compliance with this request. I think you
ought to know, however, for the very reason he
gave for withholding it from you, if for no other."

"What was that?" I asked.

"He seemed to think your husband might attribute your misfortune to his influence."

"I do not know who should ever think that," I
said in surprise, "unless it were Mr. Dickson."

"And that is precisely who it was," said the
Professor. "He said that your husband would
never have gone into the business but for his

representations, and he feared you might attribute your loss to him."

"But he loses as well as we," I said, in something of surprise.

"Yes, but he says *that* is different. He did not embark in the business by another's persuasion."

"And he could spare thought from his own losses to think of remedying ours?" I said thoughtfully.

The Professor only replied,

"He has too much energy not to repair his own also."

CHAPTER XIX.

THE PLACE OF SAPPHIRES.

PAUL recovered slowly. The doctor gave his illness a learned name, which he explained to mean a nervous prostration resulting from care or overwork and culminating in congestion. Ah me! I well knew that both care and overwork had conspired to bring my Cæsar low. He lay in a strange torpor for many days. He was not delirious, but just oblivious to all that was about him. This gradually wore off, and he came, little by little, to notice things again. The doctor said it was important that he should be kept from any excitement or anxiety as long as possible. So I just hovered about his bed all the time when he was awake, making myself as bright and cheery as possible so that he could not have gloomy thoughts. What with the knowledge of our marvelous deliverance and of my husband's silent devotion and hope for his future, this was no hard task for me to perform. For a few days I was successful. He would follow my every motion, obey each word and look, and seemed to think it quite sufficient for him to see me happy. Then he began to grow restless and ask questions as to what had occurred, and I could see he was dwelling upon our old trouble again. So I told him as carefully as I could that the mortgage was all paid off and the future bright to us once more. Then I would let him ask no more questions that day, but kept on telling him how happy I was and how I loved him better than ever before, until he went off to sleep from very weariness at my senseless chatter, I think, though there was a happy light on his slumbering face which I had not seen there in a long time before. Thus, day by day, we told him a little, until he knew all that had happened during his illness.

Then he told us how he had come in on that terrible night, found the notice, and in his despair had been tempted to do what he had very often thought of doing for my sake. He said he could think of no other way to relieve me from the pinchings of poverty which he could not bear that I should endure. He did not desire to do it to escape the pains, privations, or burdens of life himself; he had no fear of them, he said; but simply to endow me with comfort once more. He

had long meditated this course, and had determined to adopt it whenever it became necessary
to prevent the sacrifice of the dear old plantation,
the Grove. He had taken the pistol from the
drawer and was standing at the desk when, he
said, he seemed to hear my voice, and looking over
his shoulder towards the door of my room he
thought he saw me coming in my night dress to
prevent his carrying out his intention. He
thought he must act quickly or I would interrupt
him. Then came the explosion and unconscious-
ness. When he partially recovered the power of
thought it was only in a dreamy, half-conscious
way. He thought he was dead—that he had died
from the wound he had given himself—that the
pain he felt in his head was caused by that, and
his only anxiety was about the insurance money.
He had been fearful all the time while he was con-
templating the act that the company might refuse
to pay it on account of his having died by his own
hand. Then he seemed to hear me say I had got
the money, and from that instant his mind was at
rest. He slept undisturbed after that, with only
a dim idea that he was dead, and that what he
heard and sometimes saw about him was only a
dream of a past life.

Of course, he ratified the sale of the cabinet and was wheeled into the room every day, as soon as he became strong enough, to watch the Professor as he packed it for transportation. We were afraid he would regret its removal; but he declared he had never enjoyed its collection as he did the removal of it. He was anxious that others should see and enjoy its advantages as well as himself.

When the packing was almost completed and the old shelves nearly bare or removed, and the room filled with crowded cases instead, we were all in the room—the Professor, Paul and I. The Professor was picking over a heap of unassorted specimens in the corner farthest from where the desk had stood. All at once he uttered an exclamation of surprise and took something to the window for closer examination.

After a moment he gave a long low whistle, as he often did when he found something unusually fine or unexpected. Paul smiled. He was very much pleased and flattered to have so learned a man as the Professor find so many fine specimens in his collection.

"What have you found?" he asked.

"What have I found?" echoed the Professor,

half laughing. "The queerest thing in the whole collection. What do you think I have found?"

"I am sure I could not guess," said my husband.

"I should think not!" said the Professor. "It is a specimen you did not dream I would find. In fact, you did not know it was here."

"Oh! that cannot be. Paul knows everything there is here," I said eagerly.

"Come and see if you think he knew this," he replied.

I ran over to the window where he stood with my work in my hand. He held out towards me a dull rough stone covered with dust and having a queer metallic-looking excrescence toward one end.

"Well, what is it?" I exclaimed impatiently.

"What is it? Why it is that ball which your precious husband yonder tried to put through his head!"

"Let me see it," said Paul in a low tremulous tone.

We went across the room and stood silent and solemn about Paul's chair while he examined it. He looked at it a long time and then handed it back to the Professor, while he took my hand and

pressed it to his lips. I think there were tears
in all our eyes, but I was afraid the excitement would be too much for Paul, so I said
quickly,

"That is *mine*, Professor. You did not buy
that."

He caught my motive at once and said with a
queer grimace:

"Sold and delivered, madame."

Paul laughed; and I, determined to divert his
thoughts still more, sprang forward to where the
Professor sat and said, "But I will have it," and
tried to take it from him. He held it off with
one hand and laughed as he caught me by the
arm with the other and held me at a distance. I
remembered how roughly he had seized my arm
once before and could not resist the temptation
for a joke.

"Let go, sir!" I cried angrily. "You hurt my
arm!"

He released me in amazement and I went and
stood beside Paul in pretended anger.

"I am sure, Mrs. Dewar," said the Professor in
the most utter confusion—

"Pshaw, Sue," said Paul, "you must be mistaken."

"It cannot be—I cannot—" stammered the Professor.

"Look there, sir!" I said, throwing back my open sleeve and showing him the finger-marks he had left there days before. You should have seen his incredulous surprise.

"You do not mean to say, Mrs. Dewar—"

"Indeed I do mean to say, Professor Ware, that you and no one else left those marks upon my arm," I interrupted.

Then I went and stood beside Paul again. He looked at me in surprise, and took my hand in his, and said:

"Why, Cousin Sue!"

"I beg your pardon, I am sure, a thousand times," said the Professor earnestly.

"And I," said I, going over to him, "have *thanked* you a thousand times for doing it, and now thank you again;" and as I spoke I reached up and kissed him while the tears ran down my face and the laughter bubbled hysterically from my lips. I had never thanked the Professor before and could do it in no other way then. You should have seen how surprised those two men were. Then I told them how and when it was done, and the scene closed with a good deal of laughter and some crying. They held each other's hands a long time, trying every little subterfuge they could invent to choke back the tears or hide them, while their lips quivered and their tones were tremulous and tender. I stood by them, hardly knowing how many arms were around me, laughing amid my tears, glad that Paul was alive, grateful to the friend who had saved him, and thankful to the Power which had sent that bullet off to waste its baleful force upon that stone instead of shattering the life in which my own was bound up. I was proud too of those great tender-hearted boys by whom I stood, and glad indeed to be the wife of one and friend of another so true and pure as they were—two kindred souls with the likeness of brothers and the unlikeness of genius stamped upon them.

" Well," said the Professor at length, " I think I must let you have this specimen for getting me out of that difficulty so pleasantly."

He had held the stone in his hand all the time, and now the scientist overcame the man, and he said meditatively :

" I wonder what it is.   Have you any objection to my breaking it ?"—to me.

" Oh none at all, only let me have the bullet to

keep Paul in subjection with hereafter," I said, laughing.

He took a hammer and tried to break it, but it was very stubborn. He began to peer at it with unusual interest. At length he laid it on a large block of wood and struck it a heavy blow near where the ball was sticking to it. The lead fell off with a scale of the stone attached. It had broken where there was a flaw, but of the whole stone, which was as large as my hand, a piece not larger than a pea had been separated by all his efforts.

It was of a peculiar ruddy hue, as if the flame which ages ago had liquefied its particles were yet imprisoned in its crystal depths; a deep, soft, mysterious glow as if some sad, dark secret of its fervid prison-house, some tale of love and blood which happened in the days of chaos, were pent up in its glowing heart.

"What!" said the Professor in surprise, when he saw it. He went to the window and examined it more thoroughly. Then he came back to Paul and asked very seriously,

"Do you know where this came from?"

"Let me see," said Paul, taking it in his hand.

No sooner did he feel its weight and look at its

general outline than his face brightened and he said.

"Oh yes. I remember it well. There was a piece of land belonging to my father's estate up in the mountains, which had to be sold after his death. So I had it run out and advertised; but as no one wanted it, thinking it only good to hold the world together and money being scarce at that time, I had a friend bid it in for Sue at ten dollars for the whole lot. I found this when we were surveying the land. I remember noticing its peculiar shape and extraordinary weight and thinking I would study it up when I got home. What do you take it to be?"

"It is a very fine specimen of corundum," answered the Professor.

"Corundum!" said Paul with curious interest. "Do you think so?"

"I have no doubt of it, and remarkably perfect and fine, too. I think it would polish diamonds," said the Professor.

"But I did not know that any of it was to be found in this country," said Paul.

"There have been some isolated specimens," said the Professor, "and now I think of it, all or nearly all of them have been found in this State.

There may be more where you found this : if so, it is valuable. You know, of course, to what it is akin. It is but a step from corundum to sapphire and the ruby. If there are large deposits of it one may look almost to a certainty to find more or less of these crystals. I should not be surprised, if this very specimen were properly cut and worked, to find a perfect crystal ruby, without a flaw in its heart."

"I could go to the very spot where I found it," said Paul meditatively.

"Now, let me tell you what to do," said the Professor. "You know, you must get away from here as soon as you can. Suppose you go up and see if you can find any more of these pebbles. If you do, send for me and we will see what we can make out of it. There may be a good thing in it, who knows ?"

The Professor went home with the cabinet the next day. The factory was sold for the debts of the business soon afterwards, but the dear old Grove was safe, saved by the ancient Mound-Builders, who had slept for so many ages in our Mamelon ! Paul said that the grateful antediluvians, having become aware of his loving labors in their behalf, had rewarded him a thousandfold more richly than he deserved.

He would have gone to work again at once, but the old Doctor was imperative in his requirements, which I seconded effectually; so that a decree of exile and idleness was promulgated against him for a full year. Our boy, now a great lad, was at school, and has remained there while I have led Paul a constant chase after health and idleness ever since. We went to the mountains first, and Paul soon found such specimens of corundum and sent such accounts to Professor Ware that he came down post haste from New York, and almost before I knew it a company was organized, and Captain Dickson with his engines and machinery was on the ground, grinding the faulty crystals to powder to be used in polishing other jewels and hard substances— glass and the like. Every day the hopes of the great "New York Corundum Company" have been growing brighter. Paul declares he would not be surprised to learn any day that they were taking out rubies, sapphires, and I know not what other jewels there.

I found he was getting too much interested, however, and hurried him away, and have given

him little leisure for thought or occupation since.
He has taking to hunting and fishing instead.
He has gone with a party to the Everglades now;
but I am expecting his return every day, for he
declares that his year of idleness began and shall
end upon St. Valentine's day.

———

The door upon the veranda opened at this
point. The bright-eyed lady sprang up, and with
a low cry of delight bounded into a pair of
brawny arms and buried her face in a brown
forest which half hid a sunburnt visage, while a
pair of love-lighted blue eyes glanced laughingly
towards us over her ringleted head, and a well-
worn sombrero was courteously lifted in our
direction. We were rising to steal away from
the happy meeting, when she loosened her embrace and taking his arm came forward and while
the crimson love-light flashed and shone upon
her face, introduced him to the knot of charmed
girls as,

"My Paul!"

They went away in a day or two, he longing
for his unfinished book, which had lain for a year

untouched, and she yearning for her country home and absent boy, now that time and idleness had restored her lord.   But I venture there is not one who heard the tale that does not count "Cousin Sue and her Paul" the happiest pair whom St. Valentine has ever joined, and who does not hope to meet them again at Hickory Grove, now gratefully rechristened " Mamelon."

THE END.

The Fate of
MADAME LA TOUR

A Story of Great Salt Lake.

Part I.—A novel, which does for Mormonism what "Uncle Tom's Cabin" did for Slavery, and "A Fool's Errand" for the Bondage of the Freedmen in the reconstructed South—swings back the doors and lets in the revealing light of day !

"A vivid and startling picture."—*Boston Gazette.*

"The fascination of thrilling fiction."—*Cincinnati Commercial.*

"We only wish every cultivated woman could read it."—*Chicago Inter-Ocean.*

"A very valuable book, bearing upon its every page the impress of trustworthiness and sincerity."—*Cleveland Herald.*

"It may be that the facts here presented will have some effect upon the conscience of a nation too long indifferent."—*New York Tribune.*

"Gives fresh and breezy pictures of pioneer life, and portrays the ideas, principles, and modes of the Mormons, showing the strange and curious ramifications of that remarkable system of government, and giving the key to many puzzling questions."—*Detroit Free Press.*

"Not only literature but statesmanship of a high order. . . handled with remarkable skill, delicacy, and reserve, and marked throughout by a temperateness of language and a reserve of feeling . . . The story itself fires the imagination."—*Literary World* (Boston).

"Thrilling enough to interest the most exacting lover of fiction, while solemn enough in its facts and in its warnings to engage the attention of the most serious statesmen."—*The Critic* (N. Y.)

Part II.—An Appendix giving a concise *History of Utah* from 1870 to 1881: completion of Pacific railroads ; incoming of Gentiles ; opening of Mines ; clash of Christianity with Mormonism ; first Gentile Church ; Mission Work ; Hebrews and Catholics ; Utah Legislature ; Woman Suffrage ; Need of Schools and free Education ; Polygamous Marriages in 1880 ; the 70,000 Mormons in Arizona, Colorado, Idaho, Wyoming, and Nevada ; in short, a compact volume of information on that which is rapidly rising to be *the* question of the day.

"An Appendix of many pages bristles with information to parallel the narrative's fiction."—Rochester *Rural Home.*

"The Appendix to the volume constitutes a work by itself. We sincerely hope every one of our readers will peruse it."—Detroit *Commercial Advertiser.*

"A most valuable part is the Appendix of seventy pages, filled with historical statements confirmatory of the novelist's assertions."—*St. Paul Pioneer-Press.*

"A trustworthy history of Mormonism. . . Never have the mysteries of Mormonism been more skillfully unraveled, never have the sympathies of the reader been more intensely aroused."—*Providence Journal.*

Extra English Cloth. Price, $1.00.

Uniform with "A Fool's Errand."

STOWE, HARRIET BEECHER.

DOMESTIC TALES.

My Wife and I; or, Harry Henderson's History.
A Novel. *Illustrated.* Cloth, $1.50. (63d thousand.)

We and our Neighbors: The Records of an Unfash-
ionable Street. A Novel. (A Sequel to "My Wife and I.")
Illustrated. Cloth, $1.50. (53d thousand.)

Pink and White Tyranny. A Society Novel. One
of Mrs. Stowe's capital hits, in which, through a bright attractive story, she shows the follies of self-seeking and self-
pleasing in a young and charming woman, who, by the
tyranny of beauty, always managed to have her own way,
and was miserable in consequence. *Illustrated.* Cloth, $1.50.

Poganuc People: Their Loves and Lives. A Novel.
Illustrated. Cloth, $1.50. (*Recent.*) In the style of early
New England scene and character, in which Mrs. Stowe is so
inimitable. As "Oldtown Folks" was said to be founded on
Dr. Stowe's childhood memories, so this is drawn from some
of the author's own reminiscences, and has all the brightness
of genuine portraiture.

"It is long since we have had a story from Mrs. Beecher Stowe which we have so thoroughly enjoyed. As the Americans say, it is 'good all round.'"--*London Times.*

"A fertile, ingenious, and rarely gifted writer of the purely American type, doing for the traditions of New England, and its salient social features, the same sort of service that Scott rendered to the Scotch and the history and scenery of his native land; that Dickens performed for London and its lights and shadows, its chronic abuses of every sort; the same service that Victor Hugo has done for Paris, in all its social strata. Mrs. Stowe still keeps the field and her harvests ever grow. She works a vein of increasing luster."— *Titusville* (Pa.) *Herald.*

N.B.—Mrs. Stowe's Domestic Tales (the above-
named four Novels) are also issued in uniform style, in a
box, and sold *in that form only* at **$5 the set.**

STOWE, HARRIET BEECHER.—*continued.*

RELIGIOUS BOOKS.

Footsteps of the Master: Studies in the Life of Christ. Especially appropriate to the Church Seasons—Christmas, Lent, Easter, etc. With Illustrations and Illuminated Titles. 12mo. Choicely bound for Gift purposes. Extra Cloth, beveled. Price, $1.50.

"A very sweet book of wholesome religious thought."—*N. Y. Evening Post.*
"A congenial field for the exercise of her choice literary gifts and poetic tastes, her ripe religious experience, and her fervent Christian faith. A book of exceptional beauty and substantial worth."—*Congregationalist* (Boston).

Bible Heroines : Narrative Biographies of Prominent Hebrew Women in the Patriarchal, National and Christian Eras. Royal Octavo. *Elegantly Illustrated* in Oil Colors, with copies of Famous Paintings. Richly bound in cloth, $2.75 ; gilt edges, $3.25.

"The fine penetration, quick insight, sympathetic nature, and glowing narrative, which have marked Mrs. Stowe's previous works, are found in these pages, and the whole work is one which readily captivates equally the cultivated and the religious fervent nature."— *Boston Commonwealth.*

NEW JUVENILES.

A Dog's Mission, and Other Tales. Small Quarto. *Illustrated.* Cloth, extra. $1.25.

ALSO NEW AND ENLARGED EDITIONS OF

Queer Little People. A Book for Young Folks. *Illustrated.* Small 4to. $1.25.

"In the list of qualities belonging to Mrs. Stowe's versatile genius, her power of entertaining the young is not the least remarkable. Her productions in this line are original, racy, and healthful in a high degree. Her skill in allegory is, we think, unrivaled among the writers of our day.
'Queer Little People' is a collection of stories about domestic or familiar animals, told in most captivating style, and conveying, with marvelous ingenuity and power, lessons which the aged as well as the young might thankfully receive."—*American Presbyterian.*

Little Pussy Willow. *Copiously Illustrated.* Small 4to. $1.25.

"A girl's story with a moral, and with many delightful touches of New England scenery and domestic life. The story has all the familiar charm of Mrs. Stowe's simpler tales, which are always her best."—*Springfield Republican.*
"The very sweetest, prettiest child's book. It seems as if Mrs. Stowe's genius was just fitted for this work, so exquisitely has she created her country maiden ; and the illustrations are very beautiful."—*Christian Register* (Boston).

PUBLISHED BY FORDS, HOWARD, & HULBERT,

27 Park Place, New York.

THE GREAT INDIAN NOVEL!

PLOUGHED UNDER:

THE STORY OF AN INDIAN CHIEF.

TOLD BY HIMSELF.

With a Spicy Introduction about Indians,

By INSHTA THEAMBA ("Bright Eyes," of the Poncas).

16mo, Cloth, with decorative cover design from Crawford's Statue of "The Indian." $1.

"Something unique in literature. . . . It will sustain much the same relation to pending questions of Indian Policy as 'Uncle Tom's Cabin' sustained to slavery and anti-slavery agitation."—*Chicago Standard.*

"A story of the early impressions, experiences, and ideas of a young Indian chief, embodying many of the customs, usages, and legends of the red men, descriptions of hunts, battles, and incidents of many kinds, all interesting and all authentic. It presents their own notions of things, largely in their own words, and in the graphic guise of fiction makes known many significant facts, and depicts many characteristic fancies of theirs not familiar to the public."—*Providence* (R. I.) *Star.*

"The story is full of the interest of life, love, and adventure among these strange people, and contains much food for thought among our own intelligent and 'civilized' citizens. It gives a graphic picture of the Indian as he is—good and bad, like the rest of the world—and portrays the beauties of our 'Indian policy,' with its effect on the fortunes and its impression on the mind of a genuine red man. Such a showing of hidden facts is needed, and the public will welcome it, coming in such attractive form."—*New York Commercial Advertiser.*

"The writer has a keen sense of the satire of situations. . . . It is to be hoped that 'Ploughed Under' will follow fast in the footsteps of 'A Fool's Errand' and 'Bricks without Straw.' It is as true of it as of them, that a mighty purpose to show up wrongs, backed by an array of facts and incidents drawn from actual life, has a tremendous force in opening people's eyes to truth, and making them think rightly."—*The Critic.*

DATE DUE

GAYLORD   PRINTED IN U S.A